CATCH YOU ON THE FLIP SIDE

LEE KVERN

Enfield & Wizenty (an imprint of Great Plains Publications)
320 Rosedale Ave
Winnipeg, MB R3L 1L8
www.greatplains.mb.ca

Great Plains Publications gratefully acknowledges the financial support provided for its publishing program by the Government of Canada through the Canada Book Fund; the Canada Council for the Arts; the Province of Manitoba through the Book Publishing Tax Credit and the Book Publisher Marketing Assistance Program; and the Manitoba Arts Council.

Lee Kvern thanks the Canada Council for their generous grant that made this book possible.

Design & Typography by Electric Monk Media
Printed in Canada by Friesens

Library and Archives Canada Cataloguing in Publication

Title: Catch you on the flip side / Lee Kvern.
ımes: Kvern, Lee, 1957- author.
ıtifiers: Canadiana (print) 20240537718 | Canadiana (ebook) 20240537726
I 9781773371320
ıftcover) | ISBN 9781773371337 (EPUB)
LCGFT: Novels.
ion: LCC PS8621.V47 C38 2025 | DDC C813/.6—dc23

RONMENTAL BENEFITS STATEMENT

ins Press saved the following resources by
pages of this book on chlorine free paper
00% post-consumer waste.

ENERGY	SOLID WASTE	GREENHOUSE GASES
4	28	3,630
ON BTUs	POUNDS	POUNDS

ıade using the Environmental Paper Network
on visit www.papercalculator.org

Canada

2017

THE BOSS

Grizzly bear #122, "The Boss," sits in the alpine forest in the late night. The Boss because he's bad ass and clocks in at 650 pounds. He's eaten a bear black, got struck by a train and lived. Behind The Boss, the sharp violet peaks of the Three Sisters cut into the dark sky. The moon is at half mast with the shimmering lights of Canmore below. Tomorrow The Boss will descend the Three Sisters for the third day in a row and brazenly eat the July crab apples in the backyards of the town's residents. He will bluff charge them if necessary to take advantage of the food source. Parks Canada may have to relocate or kill him for the welfare of the elite town below where movie stars mix with international mountain climbers.

The road up to the lookout is deserted. The Boss sees the headlights of the utility vehicle as it pulls off the road and stops. The driver cuts the engine and squints through his windshield to make out the shadow landscape beyond. Bear #122 retreats into the beetle-infested woods and watches.

The man gets out of his vehicle and walks the perimeter of the abandoned road. No sleeping truckers in sight, no Mercedes Benz Sprinters parked off road, no random pup tents pitched in the dark forest. Yet something feels off. He inhales the air, smells nothing but Rocky Mountains and dead pine trees. To be certain, he smokes a full cigarette in the cool dark, then crushes the butt beneath his heel. He scoops up the butt and surrounding gravel, which he deposits into his shirt pocket. He was never here.

He goes around to the back of the utility vehicle and pulls the woman out. She's wrapped in the clear poly sheeting that house painters use. He's tall and buff, she's not. He easily lifts her and carries her into the shadow landscape with the shovel he purchased from the Garden Centre at Home Depot. He smells her lilac perfume mixed with three days of being in the back of his vehicle. The Boss raises his muzzle in the red copse of dead pines and sniffs the Sister air filled with something new, something foreign. He watches the man dig the coarse mountain loam, not unlike how The Boss digs for roots and tubers, unearths the occasional shrieking gopher from its underground home.

When the man is finished, he rolls the woman into the shallow rut. He can see her stunning face through the poly sheeting. He thinks about turning her over but doesn't. Instead, he shovels the silty loam over her body and stands sweating in the mountain air. He lights a cigarette, can't shake the feeling that he's being watched. He's spooked. He heads back to the vehicle. The Three Sisters' violet silhouettes are a jagged trifecta against the black sky. Then he remembers the Tahitian black pearl earrings he bought the woman.

He climbs out and goes back to the shallow rut, doesn't bother with the Home and Garden shovel this time, uses his hands to unearth her. He slits the clear poly open with his car keys, grazes his hand over the inflamed marks he inflicted on her neck, tucks the red hair that he loved behind her small ear. He didn't mean it, but that doesn't change the outcome. He sits back on his haunches, feels his remorse and exhaustion at the same moment. He leans back over her and pauses, wavering between moral and monster. Then, without bothering to unclasp the Tahitian black pearls, he rips them brutally through her velveteen earlobes. He rises and tucks the earrings in the same pocket as his cigarette butt. She owes him that and so much more.

The Boss waits until the man's headlights disappear down the abandoned road. He emerges and crosses the night plain, easily digs the woman up from the shallow channel with his four-inch claws, then drags her small body back into the dead forest. Bear #122 will have no need to descend the Three Sisters tomorrow for the town crab apples. He will survive another season.

BAGONG SILANG, PHILIPPINES 1983

I'M A PIG FARMER

The two soldiers came in the evening long after Rolando Galman laid down his shovel and his common-law-wife Lina Santos had secured the pigpen. Rolando and Lina walked back to the house, arm-in-arm, the sweltering heat of the day relentless even in the black of the archipelago night. No lights in the distance, so remote was their farm. Rolando did not bother to close the door of their concrete house. He felt a sense of pride, of cement ownership when most houses in the isolated community were constructed of wood and straw.

"Huff and puff and blow their houses down," Lina said, "but not ours."

She pulled Rolando to her in the open doorway, a briefhug after a long day. The musk of perspiration and pig pong on his body matched the tang on hers. The faint perfume of ylang-ylang that bordered the northside of their rice field hung in the air. They heard the car before they saw the dual headlights bouncing along the unpaved road. No car entered the remote farming community of Bagong Silang without the residents knowing. One rutted road in, the same one out. Lina gazed up at Rolando in the dark. He released her, kept his calloused hand in hers.

"Stay inside, Lin," he said. "Ayos lang." *It's fine.*

He kissed her sweat-glazed forehead. She stayed inside and shut the door. The sudden presence of cars and strangers in the dead of night made her edgy. She palmed the tiny cross hanging around her neck. From their open bedroom window, she watched Rolando wave the car forward.

"Galman?" the taller soldier asked, exiting the car. He was dressed in tan military fatigues. President Marcos's personal army if they were coming to see him at this hour. Rolando stood taller in the night.

"We know who you are," the smaller of the soldiers said before Rolando could affirm his identity.

"Who am I?" Rolando asked.

Rolando pulled a pack of cigarettes out from his shirt pocket and offered them to the soldiers.

"What brand?" the smaller soldier asked.

"Hope Luxury," Rolando said, rolling the name off his smiling lips.

"Menthol is not my thing," the smaller soldier said.

Rolando extracted one for himself and the taller soldier. Lighting both, they blew the cool menthol out in the evening air. In the dark, Rolando felt the intensity of the smaller soldier, who bristled with efficiency and cruelty.

"You know who you are," the smaller soldier said. They stood in the sprawl of Rolando's lush rice field, with its row of fragrant ylang-ylang whose large yellow blooms Rolando sold to perfume manufacturers visible on the dark horizon.

"I'm a pig farmer," Rolando said. The taller soldier laughed, the small man did not.

"We need you to do something for us," the small man said.

"You personally?"

The two soldiers glanced at one another.

"Someone needs you to do something," the taller man said.

"Well, that's much less vague," Rolando said. The shorter man handed Galman a tan canvas bag.

"Open it," he ordered.

Rolando saw the .357 Magnum, a bundle of money, and a neatly folded pale blue shirt with navy trousers. A uniform of some sort, though there weren't any discernible badges on it.

He looked at the taller, more affable man, who was more likely to explain. He didn't.

"He's coming back," the smaller soldier said.

"Who is coming back?"

"We'll let you know when and where," said the small man.

"Do I have a choice?" Rolando asked. He knew he didn't, but he waited for an answer anyway.

"Someone will come for you in a couple days. Early. Be ready. Bring the gun."

Neither soldier asked him if he knew how to fire the gun. He didn't. The ebb and flow of money from previous unexpected visits had nothing to do with the weight of the .357 Magnum in the canvas bag. He had an intelligent nature, was remarkably good with names, and never forgot an ominous face. People in certain political groups paid good money for his keen mind. He had no need for firearms on his watch.

"Kiss Lina," the taller soldier told him while glancing towards Lina watching from the bedroom window. The soldier flicked his down-to-the-bit cigarette off into the saturated field. Menthol and burnt cotton filter mixed with the bitter orange scent of the ylang-ylang trees.

"I'm a pig farmer," Rolando said again. The soldiers didn't buy it.

"Kiss her a lot," said the smaller soldier, a cruel grin across his dark face.

"Fuck you and the Marcos Mercedes that you rode in on," Rolando said.

President Ferdinand and his first lady, Imelda Marcos, drove custom Mercedes Benzes inside the Malacañang Palace where they resided. Their elevators were specially fitted to accommodate the cars. Rolando gazed across the field at the dark silhouette of his neighbour's horse and cart, their only mode of transportation which made the twenty-five miles south to Manila a long journey. Saliva rose at the back of Rolando's throat, but he suppressed the urge to spit.

Do it now if you have the balls, he dared the soldiers silently. The smaller soldier snickered at him. It was already done. They knew Lina's name. She was his collateral damage.

Rolando lit another Hope Luxury with the previous cigarette and stood in his green rice field long after the soldiers disappeared into the night. Rolando knew the price of concrete. This day was always coming, no matter what. He walked the edges of his property. Lina's small face peered out the open bedroom window. He held her anxious gaze while he smoked and then returned to the house.

"Magandang balita," he told Lina.

She couldn't see how two of Marcos's goons visiting in the dead of the night meant *good news*.

"I've got work," he said and showed Lina the bundled money, the pale blue collared shirt and navy trousers. He didn't show her the gun. She counted the bundled money slowly. The more pisos she counted, the more Rolando's jaw tensed.

"This much," she said. She felt a knot in the pit of her childless belly. Their usual lovemaking was slow and careful, calculated always to avoid pregnancy. Their existence was precarious under the extended years of martial law that the Marcos regime had only recently lifted. The economy flat-lined hard. Foreign investors had pulled out of the tumultuous country one-by-one until there was nothing left. Lina understood what the money represented but didn't inquire further. Better not to know the details. The cars, the visitors that came to see Rolando at all hours. His sharp, almost uncanny Rolodex of ministers and generals, senators and politicians, influential businessmen, their faces, their names, their power positions. Lina felt the stirrings of an imminent revolution in her aching muscles at night. What she didn't know was that Rolando would be a key player.

"Could we..." she asked Rolando in their dark kitchen now.

He shook his head, stopped her mid-sentence.

"When?" she asked.

"A couple days."

She took Rolando's pig-farmer hands and led him to their single bed where she made feverish, sweat-laden love with him. Not careful, not slow, but ardent. Lina's body was attuned to some fanatical purpose that Rolando could not guess. Nor did he care. Afterward, he lay awake in the night until the morning sun permeated the hot air of their room. No longer would he lie awake and despair at the lack of work. For Lina, he wished for a child. But who could bring a child into this? Hard not to envision the entire country on its proverbial knees like the impoverished farmers living in houses that a huff and stiff puff could knock over. Rolando couldn't think straight.

"Three days, four days," he whispered into the dark. Lina didn't answer. His anger rose at the audacity of the Marcos's men threatening him with the mention of Lina's name. He knew the real threat was the former beauty queen, Imelda Marcos, dubbed the Iron Butterfly. Her shoe collection took up entire rooms in the palace while parts of his community went without. The neighbour's wife wore rubber shoes. The swelling outrage that Rolando sensed every time he made the journey to Manila. He didn't have to think about that anymore. He would wear his Sunday best leather shoes as a pakyu to the Iron Butterfly. *Fuck you.*

LOS ANGELES, USA
1983

NO DOUBT

International correspondent Ken Kashiwahara surveyed the crystal chandeliers that swayed in the Ambassador Hotel. The Greco-Roman swank of the hotel lobby included gold columns that reached from the vaulted ceiling down to the extravagant palm frond carpet. Large bouquets of fresh white gardenias, apricot-coloured dahlias, pink-freckled lilies and blue hydrangeas marked each pillar. The air was flush with the fragrance of jasmine that masked the cigarette and cigar smoke of journalists and correspondents from around the world who waited in the lobby of one of the most prestigious hotels in the US. Ken spied the ornate gold baby grand piano in the corner and the pink velvet chairs the journalists sat on. Stomping grounds for countless Hollywood legends, heads of state—at least seven US presidents had stayed here.

The Ambassador Hotel was infamous for the assassination of Robert Kennedy. The same hotel in which Kennedy had won his state primary in his bid for the American presidency. The same hotel in which Kennedy had met his fate; the zealous man who jumped out from behind a silver ice machine.

Ken's brother-in-law, Senator Benigno Aquino Jr., affectionately known as Ninoy, walked through the front door of the Ambassador lobby, no entourage, no security.

"I want to go downstairs," Ninoy said, even though the scrum of journalists had risen from their chairs and were waiting for him. He nodded warmly in their direction, held up his finger for a moment.

"I covered this story years back," Ken Kashiwahara told Ninoy as they rode the elevator to the basement kitchen one floor below. The kitchen was empty, the kitchen staff possibly out running errands or taking a break in between the lunch and dinner service.

Ninoy stood in reverent silence where the police outline of Kennedy's body remained eerily etched on the cement floor from some fifteen years earlier. Ninoy took Ken's arm. Neither man said anything.

Seventeen-year-old busboy Juan Romero shook hands with a victorious Robert Kennedy, who not ten minutes prior had claimed the state win in the Democratic presidential primary upstairs. The boy was eager to congratulate him. He'd delivered room service to Kennedy earlier in the week and had not forgotten the way Kennedy treated him—with decency, equality, respect. Then the lone shooter, who stepped out from behind the ice machine and fired eight shots from his .22-calibre rifle.

Juan Romero had held the dying Kennedy in his arms amid the ensuing chaos. No one knew who had been shot. Juan spotted the hole in Kennedy's head. Robert's hot Irish blood seeped out onto both of them. Juan knew it was serious. He removed the red-beaded rosary from the pocket of his kitchen whites and placed it in Kennedy's clenched fist. If Kennedy hadn't paused to shake his hand, would he still be alive?

"Is everybody okay?" Kennedy gazed up at Juan in the Ambassador kitchen. The red shock of blood spread onto Juan's white uniform.

"Yes," Juan reassured Kennedy. "Everybody's okay."

"Everything's going to be okay," Kennedy said, ever the political optimist. Then he shut his hazel eyes and rested in the boy's arms. Juan cradled his head, and that image caught by a *LIFE* photographer was seared into the mind of every American thereafter: Robert Kennedy's demise on the concrete floor of a subterranean kitchen in the arms of a Jesus-loving busboy.

"You're my hero, Juan Romero!" people yelled out to him on the streets of Los Angeles. People came in droves to the Ambassador Hotel to get a picture with him.

"I wanted to protect him from the cold concrete," Juan Romero had told Ken Kashiwahara after the assassination. He'd gone to school the next day with Kennedy's blood crusted under his fingernails that he refused to wash off. Ken would not forget that detail.

"Everything's going to be okay," Ninoy said in response to the faded yellow outline on the concrete floor and the stricken look on Ken's face. He knew that Ken's mind would turn to considering Ninoy's fate.

Ken Kashiwahara looked at his brother-in-law, the official opposition leader and arch opponent of President Ferdinand Marcos. He feared for Ninoy. After three years of self-exile in the US, Ninoy was going back to the Philippines. The only man positioned to unseat Marcos in the upcoming election was Ninoy. But would it be in life or death? Ken didn't know the answer to that question yet. He pulled Ninoy away from Kennedy's outline and they stood quietly waiting for the service elevator to take them above ground to the waiting journalists.

Aquino sat at the marble table with Ken and their friend Jim Laurie, an ABC journalist; a select group of smoking, day-drinking journalists would accompany him back to the Philippines in four days.

"Senator Benigno S. Aquino, Jr." a Canadian journalist said in a bid for Aquino's attention.

"Just call me Ninoy."

Aquino waved his hand at the young man, a friendly gesture. A former journalist himself, Ninoy was easy-going, comfortable with the press. The world was watching, and Aquino needed to be sure it was paying attention. That, more than anything else, was the key to his safe return. His final bid to negotiate a peaceful "stepping down" of the autocratic regime. He hoped that President Ferdinand Marcos would grant him a private audience and allow him access to the Philippine media.

"Why now? Why go back now?" Jim Laurie asked.

Marcos had forbidden his return, threatened foreign airlines with loss of landing rights in the Philippines if anyone dared transport Benigno Aquino Jr. Ninoy used a travel alias: Marcial Bonifacio. *Marcial* for martial law under the Marcos regime. *Bonifacio* for Fort Bonifacio where Ninoy spent seven years imprisoned in a single, windowless room—a bed, a desk, no windows.

Ninoy glanced at his brother-in-law. Ken nodded solemnly.

"Why go back now?" Ninoy repeated Jim's question.

"Because I once courted Imelda Marcos?" he said to Jim, a grin on his congenial face. "Because Ferdinand and I were in the same fraternity way back when? Because I'm a radical rich guy?"

Tongue-in-cheek, Aquino was a provocateur known and loved by his fellow Filipino women and men. Aquino gestured in the direction of the gilded baby grand. A rich joke on Ninoy's part.

"Seven years in detainment broke me financially. Broke my heart, too," Ninoy said, rubbing his chest with his fist. "Literally."

A blocked valve threatened what little he had left. He'd been allowed to leave the country only because Imelda Marcos feared that if Ninoy died of a heart attack in their custody, he'd be akin to the martyred saint of Christ. She knew the Filipino people would rise against her. Reluctantly, she granted Ninoy passage to the US for bypass heart surgery with the provision that Aquino ceased his pointed attacks on their government—that he'd quit stirring the pot of malcontent amongst their people. He did neither. He battered them daily from US soil in newspapers and on television and at lucrative American fundraisers sending money back to the Philippines to help restore the democracy that the Marcos administration had pulled out from under them.

"I've got the eyes and ears of the world thanks to my exile in America, and Imelda Marcos, the woman I once courted, to thank for it." Ninoy laughed.

The journalists around the table gasped at the paradox of his statement. *He'd once courted the Iron Butterfly. He'd been frat brothers with Ferdinand Marco, a murderous dictator*. Ken Kashiwahara didn't gasp. Ken knew that Ninoy came from a long line of disrupters. His anti-colonist grandfather was sentenced to hang, but mercifully pardoned so he could go forth and spawn future generations of Aquino politicians. The Aquinos were the Kennedys of the Philippines. Ninoy's political father had been similarly detained in his bid for democracy before he died three years ago. Aquino's mother, Aurora, was a political activist and ardent supporter of her son. She kept the home fires burning while Ninoy was on US soil. Ninoy's wife, Corazon Aquino, was a lawyer. Soft-spoken but sharp-edged, she was brazen like her husband.

A sly grin slipped onto Ninoy's face. Never one to shy away from flamboyant rhetoric, he was a media favourite. The trick of Ninoy was that he affected everyone he met. Except it was no trick. Ninoy was the same charming, intelligent, truth-speaking man in the company of his family and friends as he was in the public eye.

His years in starless solitude had taken away his need for political power and replaced it instead with the need to wake his Filipino sisters and brothers to revolt against Marcos's regime. It was not about him anymore.

"But is it safe to go back?" Jim Laurie pushed the question forward again.

Aquino reached over and squeezed Jim Laurie's hand briefly, appreciating his genuine concern.

"Who better than an entourage of international journalists to hold President Marcos accountable to the world? Surely even Marcos wouldn't stop me? Would he?" Aquino asked. He was optimistic, but no fool. "Marcos is ill. The election is coming up. My people need me to come back now and lead," Ninoy said, quieter so that only Ken sitting next to him heard. "I need my people," he said.

Ninoy touched his chest, felt the raised scar from the surgery beneath his shirt, his healed heart beating strongly beneath.

"If I get shot in the head like Kennedy, I am not going to fall on my knees. If you get shot like that, you have a few seconds of life left," Ninoy explained to the stunned journalists. Only Ken knew where this was coming from. Kennedy's outline in the kitchen below their feet.

Who would talk about their assassination, let alone visualize it? The journalists listened in dazed silence.

"If that happens to me, I am going to fall straight down and spread my arms so the people will know I never gave up, even at the last second," Aquino said. He spread his arms wide like an eagle to demonstrate, encompassing both Ken and Jim Laurie in his genial, expansive wingspan. Afterwards, Jim Laurie's journalist remorse gnawed at him in not trying harder to dissuade his determined friend from returning to the Philippines. The same as Juan Romero's busboy regret in stopping Robert Kennedy to shake his hand.

The outline of Robert Kennedy's body one floor below was incised in Ken Kashiwahara's mind. Where would his brother-in-law's outline be? He didn't want to think about that. No one in the room did.

"What can one man do? I have no army, no money," Aquino said, his eyes like flickering stars. "I have only my indomitable spirit. The Filipino people are worth dying for." No one in the Ambassador Hotel doubted him. Spirit and worth. Both were sacred.

MANILA, PHILIPPINES
1983

WHO WORE WHAT ON THE RUNWAY?

Metro Manila. Amado Barcelona, a twenty-two-year-old baggage handler, stood outside the main terminal of the Manila Airport in his pale blue button-up shirt and navy trousers that made the tropical heat on the tarmac unbearable at times. Though the heat wasn't what he'd remember most from this Sunday. He spotted a tiny woman dressed entirely in yellow with a megaphone. She spoke to a restless crowd of thousands who waited outside the main terminal. Someone important must be coming in today. Amado lit a Marlboro and emitted a series of smoke rings, trying to break his record.

"What's up?" His baggage handler buddy J-Mar strode up to him from across the parking lot and extracted a Marlboro from Amado's pocket. Amado swiped his hand across J-Mar's black shining mohawk. J-Mar ducked and laughed. Both men were dressed identically.

"Not sure, Jejomar," Amado said. The first time they'd worked together years back, Amado had repeated *Jejomar Jejomar Jejomar* until J-Mar explained it was his mother's combined version of Jesus, Joseph and Mary. *Jesus Christ*, Amado had replied. *That's a lot to live up to*. They'd shared a laugh and never turned back. Now they had each other's back no matter what. They smoked and watched the cheering crowd. It was hard to make out what the woman in yellow was saying; the roar of the crowd overwhelmed her megaphone.

"Someone famous must be coming in today," Amado said.

"Hope it's Princess Leia!" J-Mar said. Amado laughed. They had watched *The Return of the Jedi* no less than three times at the movie theatre when it came out that summer.

"What's that about?" They glanced at Marcos's soldiers who lined the walls of the airport terminal inside.

"Maybe it's Harrison Ford," Amado said, his pale gold eyes brightening. "I'll bet Imelda Marcos would send her goons out for him."

"Hell, if that's the case, I'll carry Harrison in personally," J-Mar offered.

They both admired Han Solo and his one-man rebellion in the *Millennium Falcon* against the organized forces of the corrupt Emperor, who was not unlike Ferdinand Marcos.

"Watch this." Amado took a colossal drag, then puffed out sixteen consecutive smoke rings. He counted, like he counted everything he did (the succession of every piece of luggage he unloaded, the red lights versus the green lights on the way to work, the smoke rings he blew)—it helped pass the time of day. Where J-Mar was loose and chill, Amado was a man of precision.

"A new world record for the Marlboro Man," J-Mar hooted.

Sixteen smoke rings that would match the shots fired by the same number of soldiers on the tarmac within the next hour. They watched a heavily decorated general walk past with a civilian man who was dressed like a fellow baggage handler. J-Mar raised his chin at the man. The man stared back at J-Mar's black, shining mohawk like he'd never seen one before. Perhaps he hadn't.

"Democracy!" the tiny woman dressed in yellow with the megaphone shouted. The military man and unknown baggage handler disappeared inside the terminal. J-Mar would not remember this. Amado would.

The crowd outside erupted into a massive roar and pumped their yellow ribbon-wrapped fists in the sticky air. Amado and J-Mar joined them, raising their naked fists in solidarity, though they didn't know what for. They didn't know what the yellow meant. It didn't matter. Both felt like today was the first day of the rest of their altered lives. Amado crushed his cigarette butt on the concrete, then they slipped inside the terminal. Airport security was heavy, not uncommon in the face of high personnel flying into Manila. But it was the addition of Marcos's cold-faced, khaki-laden soldiers that made Amado catch his breath. A thousand soldiers inside the main terminal. Unheard of, even considering the peaceful crowd gathered outside. The soldiers' presence was rarely associated with anything useful. Amado was on high alert now. J-Mar walked with his head bent to hide his distinguishable mohawk.

Taipei, Taiwan. The last leg of Ninoy's journey home. Senator Aquino was clad in the same crisp white safari suit that he'd left the Philippines in three years earlier. He stepped aboard a China Airlines plane whose landing rights would be suspended in Manila in the following days for transporting him.

On the plane, Aquino sat in the second section of coach so as not to draw attention from the regular passengers while the rest of the foreign journalists sat in first-class with the Crying Lady who would also become famous for a brief period in her life.

The plane buzzed with Aquino's shimmering presence. It was hard to not know who he was on account of the coverage by the US and international press. His was the brave face of a non-violent man determined to bring down the Marcos's regime peacefully. He was flanked on either side by Ken Kashiwahara and Jim Laurie. Jim leaned forward to admire the embroidered BSA patch on Ninoy's white safari jacket.

"Does that stand for Boy Scouts of America?" Jim asked, grinning wide.

Despite the nerve-racking ten-minute delay on the runway where no one knew why they hadn't left yet, Ninoy smiled.

"Yes, my friend, that's exactly what it stands for."

Jim Laurie laughed. All three men went quiet and held their breath until the stewardess secured the airplane door and the dual engines roared to life. Not until the plane taxied out and made its rapid bid for the clear blue sky did Ninoy let his breath out.

Manila International Airport. General Perez hustled Rolando Galman through the throngs of cheering people outside. Rolando saw the tiny woman dressed in yellow with the megaphone at the head of the crowd. He recognized her immediately. Aurora Aquino. Senator Benigno Aquino's mother. She was a force to be reckoned with.

"Soon, we will be reunited with our leader," Aurora Aquino told the crowd. The people erupted into a massive roar. Ninoy's welcome home. Tie a yellow ribbon round an old oak tree. Or your fist. Rolando noticed two airline employees smoking outside the terminal. The two men pumped their fists as well. Both men were dressed in the same pale blue shirt and navy trousers that he wore. One of them had a black, shining mohawk. Hard to miss that. Now Rolando understood what the uniform meant. Now he understood who was coming home. Like the rest of the country, he knew who Senator Aquino was. Their Hope Luxury.

Would they be reunited with their leader? Rolando wasn't sure. The heft of the nickel-plated revolver in Rolando's pocket that no one—not the fortified airport security, not the thousand strong Marcos's soldiers—bothered to check when they entered the main terminal was unbearable. The General's tight face and deadly reputation were the only security pass Rolando needed. The soldiers watched Rolando shrewdly as he walked the long hall to Arrivals. Conversely, the airport security turned their heads away. The less they knew, the better. On the other hand, every single soldier at the airport that day would later testify to seeing Rolando Galman enter the airport terminal. The multiple conflicting views were pieces of a lethal puzzle that would take a decade to reassemble.

Amado Barcelona and J-Mar strode past the line of soldiers in the main terminal, went below to the ramp level breakroom and checked their shift schedule. Flight 811, Gate 8, due to arrive at 1:04 p.m.

They watched out the hangar window as the Taipei flight touched down on the far runway.

Firmly on Manila asphalt, Flight 811 taxied down the runway headed toward the main terminal. Senator Benigno Aquino heard the definitive click of two hundred seatbelts released at the same time when the plane came to a final stop at the gate. He caught a brief glimpse of the roaring crowd. Against all odds, this might work.

Then the entire plane descended on Senator Benigno S. Aquino Jr. Camera bulbs burst and flashed, video cameras rolled inside the tight cabin of the plane. The journalists peppered Ninoy with last minute questions. Jim Laurie held his tape recorder close, Ken Kashiwahara snapped pictures of his smiling brother-in-law, generous and calm in the face of the heightened, fearful media. Ken leaned into Ninoy and whispered in his ear.

"If the soldiers come for you, tell them I am your brother-in-law. That I need to go with you." Ninoy assured his brother-in-law that he would.

Jim Laurie glanced out the plane window, saw the boarding party on the tarmac. Sixteen soldiers dressed in khaki, some in blue coveralls. All heavily armed.

"Barricades and security are on," Jim told Ninoy. Jim's face was apprehensive.

"I think the very fact alone that we can land is victory enough," Ninoy said. "Everything after that's a bonus. I have promised to return, and I have returned against all odds. So that's good enough for me," Ninoy said.

"Do you think President Marcos will kill you?" a British journalist shouted over the assault of questions. The plane went dead silent to hear the answer.

"My feeling is we all must die sometime. If my fate is to die by an assassin's bullet, so be it," Aquino said. His voice wavered once, then got strong again, determined. "But I cannot be petrified by an action, or fear of an assassin and therefore stay in the corner. I must suffer with my people. I must lead them because of the responsibility given to me by our people."

Two Filipino women broke the tomb-like silence, rushed the constricted aisle of the plane and approached Ninoy. One woman kissed him on his forehead like a beloved child.

"One from the lips," the other woman said, and cupped Aquino's earnest face in her hands and kissed his smiling, laughing face. She missed and kissed Ninoy's band of white teeth instead.

"My wife is not going to like that," Ninoy said, his face flushed.

Everyone laughed. The anticipation was extraordinary for him after exile in the US. For a brief glorious moment on the plane, he was a free man. He might live to see the shimmering stars in the night sky of his homeland. He didn't know that his mother, who'd taken up the cause for democracy after Aquino's father died, was the one that led the cheering crowd. He saw the heavy presence of Marcos's military. Even though Ninoy had told only a handful of people, Marcos knew he was coming home, too. He paused and wrote down a last-minute thought for his wife and five children still in the US. *Don't come yet*, he wrote in his letter, *wait until I see what's going to happen*. Corazon had held him for too long when he'd hugged her and the children goodbye. He could still feel his wife's body against him even now in the anxious thrum of the plane. She was a brand on his like-minded soul.

Rolando Galman stood in the shade beneath the jetway with General Perez. A running van was parked on the runway. Rolando didn't know why. He spotted the same two soldiers that had come out to his farm. The taller man nodded at him, the shorter one was grim-faced, staring straight ahead like Rolando didn't exist. General Perez all but ignored him now. The tension was high on the tarmac, the plane door not yet opened.

Rolando stood with both arms stiff at his side, ready for whatever came. Airport security didn't want to see his face. Out of sight out of mind. See no evil, know no evil. *Be no evil*, Rolando decided. No one involved was getting out of this alive. He might be their fall guy, but he would not be their trigger man. Fuck Marcos, every single one of them.

The plane door opened. Five junior soldiers mounted the air stairs and paused at the entrance to locate Aquino in the coach section of the plane. The first soldier referred to a recent newspaper picture of Senator Aquino from the lobby of the Ambassador

Hotel to identify him. They pushed down the narrow aisle to get through the scrum of nervous passengers and uneasy journalists. In his seat, Aquino pulled on his bulletproof vest, although it would do him no good.

The journalists raised their 35mm cameras in the direction of the approaching soldiers. Aquino bent his head and thought of his treasured wife Corazon. He rubbed his rosary and finished a soundless prayer to the Blessed Mother.

Ninoy thought briefly of Robert Kennedy. When the soldiers reached him, Aquino smiled up at them from his seat, ever the accommodating Filipino his mother Aurora Aquino had raised him to be. The soldiers didn't smile back. Ninoy grabbed his shoulder bag, which they took from him. He even thanked them as they helped him up from his seat. Ken Kashiwahara rose at the same time.

"I'm his brother-in-law. Can I come with him?" Ken asked.

"Yes, yes," the soldiers said, not understanding. "You just stay here."

They pushed past Ken Kashiwahara with Senator Aquino in their midst. No one was allowed to exit the plane ahead of them. Ninoy was no longer smiling. The journalists' cameras filmed the solemn march out to the jetway. Everyone's faces were struck with the blaring reality of the impending situation.

Surely, they'd go straight ahead to the main terminal where thousands of Ninoy's people awaited his return? But no. A sudden change in plans. The soldiers opened the door to the air stairs. The mid-afternoon sun poured in, blinding the press and their cameras. Everything recorded after that was a bright, unsure blur. No one could be sure what happened.

It happened in the split of a second, in the flash of a blind camera, in the blink of Ninoy's eyes that required nothing more than to see the night stars of his homeland once more. His people and the stars. The freedom they all craved.

Aquino, alone, faced the group of soldiers waiting below on the tarmac. Ninoy hoped his one-man army would not fail him but then came the sobering realization.

Eto na, Ninoy thought. *This is it.*

"Pusila! Pusila!" someone yelled. *Shoot him! Shoot him!*

Rolando Galman still hadn't drawn the .357 Magnum from his pocket, nor would he.

"Ako na, ako na!" one of the soldiers behind Aquino yelled. *Let me do it.*

Then the single shot they all heard from the jetway. Amado Barcelona came across the black tarmac in his tug cart at that exact moment in time. The next fourteen seconds would mark the first day of his altered life. He saw the five soldiers on the air stairs, the man dressed in a white safari suit in their midst. The soldier's handgun pointed at the base of the man's head as they descended the stairs. Amado had no idea who the man in the safari suit was. No Harrison Ford, of that he was certain. He only saw the malevolent intent of the soldier behind the man in white, whose slate grey handgun glinted in the bright sun.

It was easy to identify later who was wearing what on the runway. The soldiers were in dark coveralls at the base of the stairs, The khaki-clad soldiers were on the air stairs, including the one who pulled the trigger of his cocked .45 and created the supersonic report of a single shot. The man in the white safari suit fell forward onto the black tarmac. Face down, Ninoy's arms were spread wide like an eagle. His presence of mind in the last seconds of his life compelled him to spread his wings and encompass his people.

The man in the white safari suit had red blood seeping from the back of his head onto his starched white collar and his useless bulletproof vest. The man, Amado learned later, was the beloved Senator Benigno Aquino Jr. Ninoy.

Amado Barcelona watched the events unfold like a man in the throes of a paralytic dream, fully cognizant of the impending threat but unable to do anything about it. He knew there was more to come. The unarmed civilian dressed in the pale blue shirt and navy trousers had talked and laughed with the khaki-clad soldiers armed with machine guns and rifles and handguns. Then a flurry and bedlam of multiple shots fired by soldiers directly into the body of the talking, laughing man. Amado arched back sharply on his tug cart like he'd been shot. He counted. Sixteen shots from sixteen soldiers.

"Jesus Christ!" Jim Laurie shouted at the crack of the single bullet they all heard but couldn't see. He pushed past the soldiers who slammed the jetway door shut. He and Ken and the group of journalists fought their way back onto the plane for a viewpoint.

"He's dead, he's dead," the Crying Lady in first-class cried.

The Crying Lady pressed her sobbing face against the tinted airplane window. Her future testimony at the first of many trials would be null and void, seemingly discredited because she'd had an unfortunate time in her life where she passed counterfeit cheques in Taipei. The Crying Lady, along with Amado Barcelona, were the only ones to see the actual shots and witness the two bodies of the men lying side-by-side on the runway before the khaki-clad soldiers dragged Aquino's body off into the idling van. A much-loved senator and a purported communist pig farmer. The Senator's face was down, his arms spread wide on the scorching tarmac. The pig farmer dressed like airport personnel was face up, his shoes blown clean off his feet. After Rolando's death, the niggling question in the subsequent trials: Why was he face up? Why hadn't he run away after he'd fired the fatal shot? Wouldn't that put him face down?

Amado had an inexplicable urge to drive his tug cart toward the Boeing 767 straight into the cold heart of the pandemonium after the volley of sixteen bullets, the screaming and crying he heard from the plane, the soldiers shouting disordered orders. Amado wanted nothing more than to reinstate the civilian's brown loafers on his feet. It was the least he could do given the sixteen soldiers, the sixteen shots. A man should die with dignity, Amado reasoned illogically. The shoes were a birthday present from his wife, Amado found out later.

Before he floored the accelerator on his tug cart and disappeared into an empty hangar, before he slipped south to the softer, looser borders to escape a murderous dictator, and before he flew to English-speaking Canada, Amado Barcelona locked his gaze with General Perez's lethal eyes in the aftershock of a feverish dream on Sunday, August 21, 1983.

ENGLISH-SPEAKING CANADA 1984

THE GREATEST OUTDOOR SHOW ON EARTH

Twenty-year-old blackjack dealer Elle surveyed the crush of players pressed outside the metal gates of the Convention Centre in downtown Calgary. Elle's face was covered in freckles, and her shoulder-length hair was a bright red that everyone commented on. *So rare! A redhead! How gorgeous. Just like Sigourney Weaver! Have you seen that movie,* Ghostbusters?

"Does the cuff match the collar?" a cheeky player inquired once, making Elle flush.

"It's just hair," Elle said, downplaying the fuss that she didn't understand.

She was flanked by her comrades-in-arms: Erik from the Netherlands. Amado Barcelona who'd recently emigrated from the Philippines (she and Amado had taken the same blackjack course last year when he'd first arrived). Regrettable Russell with whom Elle shared her Player's cigarettes in the dealers' breakroom. The reason they were all there was money. For Elle, the initial thrill of being a card dealer and the romanticized movie version of the casino was gradually stripped away by the regularity/predictability of the job itself. The same players, the same four decks of cards, the same black and white attire six days a week. Now in her second year as a dealer, Elle smoothed her black polyester tie down, then massaged her sore temples beneath her long red hair while they waited for the casino to open.

Amado came into the casino every morning prior to everyone else and vacuumed the felt tables, emptied ashtrays, put the cards in the plastic numbered shoes and placed them onto their corresponding blackjack tables.

"Do you not get enough of this fucking place during the day?" Erik had asked about Amado's early morning duties on top of his casino shifts on top of their drinking shifts at the Holiday Inn Lounge.

"I need the extra money," Amado said, his face serious. Neither Erik nor Elle pressed him further. They might have saved him if they had. Neither one of them realized the depth of his commitment until it was too late.

"Did you stay late with Erik last night?" Amado Barcelona asked. He was on the adjacent blackjack table, counting his locked chip tray to make sure it tallied up properly. He counted everything he did. He rarely smiled.

She glanced over at Amado's pale gold eyes; she had never seen the like before on a man or a woman. The kind of sad, fascinating eyes that made Elle wonder what life he'd lived prior. Like Amado held some specific brand of despair that lived far beyond anything that Elle could comprehend.

"No, I left the Holiday Inn Lounge right after you did. Went home to argue with my boyfriend about who's going to clean the bathtub. It's been three months now. I shower at the gym."

"At least you have a boyfriend." Amado half-smiled.

"Want him?" Elle offered back. "You wouldn't like him. I get home three hours after he gets off work and he's on the sofa smoking pot waiting for me to make dinner for him. Christ, I'd be better off with a roommate or a tabby cat than a boyfriend. He's all yours." Amado didn't respond.

"Why did you come to Canada? Calgary specifically?" Elle asked, changing the subject. She didn't want to complain about her temporary boyfriend.

"I saw an ad for the Calgary Stampede at the airport in Malaysia," Amado said. "I liked the look of the cowboys."

It was ten days of cowboys, bronc riders, chuckwagon races, country singing stars, pancake breakfasts and undercooked sausages combined with non-stop drinking. The whole city knew it well and, apparently, according to Amado Barcelona, so did the world.

"The Greatest Outdoor Show on Earth," Amado said to Elle, though his despondent eyes didn't reflect that. Nor had his actual experience at the Stampede lived up to the poster's promise when Erik had taken him last summer. The pair of them were decked out in ranch shirts with pearl snap buttons and tight-ass Wrangler jeans that still had the store crease in them. Overdressed, they'd wandered the softened black asphalt of the Stampede grounds in the thirty-degree Celsius heat, eaten corn dogs and mini donuts and deep-fried Mars Bars until they felt like vomiting.

"The Greatest *Indoor* Show on Earth is at the Holiday Inn Lounge," Erik said. Elle laughed, looking over at him. His hair was perfectly coiffed, dark and slicked back, while his white shirt was untucked and yellowed. His black regulation tie resembled a wad of electrical tape, while his wrinkled trousers looked like he'd spent the night in the trunk of his Chevy Impala in the Holiday

Inn parking lot again. Amado shook his head. He and Erik and Elle went there regularly after their day shifts at the casino. Only Erik took them seriously.

They both watched Regrettable Russell in the adjacent pit. His glacial eyes in combination with his acne-scarred cheeks made him less adorable than Dutch Erik in all his gory dishevelment. At least Erik shared his French Vanilla Vodka with them beneath the table at the Holiday Inn Lounge. The punk rocker bartender with Kohl black eyes at the Lounge never blinked, though surely, he was savvy to Erik.

"Stay away from that guy," Amado warned her in relation to Regrettable Russell, who stared back at Elle. Yesterday he'd sauntered past her blackjack table, not taking his polar-blue eyes off her.

"I dig redheads," he'd told Elle, which made her even more uncomfortable than the *does-the-cuff-match-the-collar* comment. Elle had glanced across the pit at Russell's wife, Liv, who was dealing blackjack. Her startling violet eyes, like Liz Taylor's, followed his every move.

"Well, maybe you should tell that to your wife, Russell," Elle had snapped back. She'd nodded her head at Liv, who wouldn't meet her gaze. Russell stood for a while longer until the owner, George Apple, walked past.

"Leave her alone, Russell," George said, waving his hand in the air. "Get back to work." Russell, 6'3" but skinny, was no match for George Apple's sturdy firefighter body. Russell wandered off without objection.

"Don't be duped, he's mapanganib," Amado said again. *Dangerous.*

Amado finished sorting his cards and adjusted the yellow woven bracelet that he never took off his left wrist.

"Does that mean something?" Elle asked.

"From a friend," Amado said.

Elle waited for more, but it didn't come.

At noon sharp, the metal gates of the Convention Centre rose sluggishly. Several players were pressed at the front: Rude Rudy, The Crier, and Billy Jacked (nicknamed for that cult movie *Billy Jack* from the 1970s). Like the movie actor Tom Laughlin, Billy Jacked wore a black cowboy hat, a beaded choker, and a leather fringed vest with no shirt underneath to show off his jacked biceps and pumped chest.

"Think he's a Stampede cowboy like us?" Amado asked Erik.

Erik shook his head.

"He's a wacked cowboy."

Billy Jacked lay down on the red paisley carpet and rolled military-style beneath the slowly rising gate like a backwards prison break. Moose, the security guard at the front, watched him with a smirk on his broad face. Sometimes he stopped him. Sometimes he let him roll. He knew Billy Jacked, like all the players, wanted first pick of the thirty blackjack tables, four roulette tables and two money wheels that only drunks and the uninitiated played. No one wanted Billy Jacked at their table. Moose rolled his eyes at Elle, who rolled her eyes at Amado, who put his hands solemnly up in the air like he'd been arrested. Elle laughed. Weird.

After the initial foot race between Rude Rudy, Billy Jacked, and The Crier, Rudy dove to secure the anchor spot on Elle's table; The Crier made his way to the roulette pit. Along with the trio of regulars, a young white guy and a Filipino woman and her adult son in dark Ray-Bans walked past their tables. Amado nodded at them.

"Sampu," Amado said in Tagalog. He didn't bother to translate that for Elle, which he usually did. He tilted his chin towards an open blackjack table in the adjacent pit.

"Does that mean *good morning*?" Elle asked.

Amado didn't answer. The trio took over the entire blackjack table.

Better not to have uncertain players when they wagered the house maximum, which they did. More control that way.

"Do you know them?" Elle asked.

Amado shook his head.

"Just nodding at my people," he said, without a trace of irony on his lips. "You don't see many of us here."

Elle looked around the casino. All people of all (legal) ages, all colours and cultures from around the world, who like Amado, had seen the "Greatest Outdoor Show on Earth" adverts and flocked here, confusing it with the casino. Whatever the case, the casino was a veritable United Nations of Ill-Tempered Players. Amado's table filled up quickly—players from every country liked him.

Wayne, their eighty-year-old pit boss, caught Elle's eye and mimed tucking in his shirt from the pit stand. Elle glanced down at hers. Wayne shook his head and nodded in Dutch Erik's direction.

"Erik, Wayne wants you to tuck your shirt in," Elle told him.

"Wayne can kiss my—" Erik said, interrupted by the group of retired firefighters who sat down at his table. A pleasant group that came in daily, they always had riveting stories of saving people from burning buildings. Saving people from themselves. More importantly, the firemen were decent people when they lost. Elle wished they'd sat at her table. Instead, she got the most difficult players, the ones with gambler hatchets to bury. Rude Rudy was on her anchor. He weighed her down daily.

Wayne, exhaling Marlboro smoke out through his nostrils, came over from the middle of the pit.

"Sharpen up, soldier," Wayne told Erik, who fanned his cards and didn't bother to look up. Nor did he tuck in his yellowed shirt. George Apple strode through the pit and after a sharp glance,

Erik relented and tucked his shirt into his rumpled trousers, then smoothed down his black apron.

Across from Elle, Regrettable Russell fanned his cards like a card shark. Not quite as slick as the magician that George Apple interviewed last month then declined to hire despite his superior blackjack skills. George had watched the magician make a black hundred-dollar chip disappear right before his management eyes.

"No," George said, firmly. "Too deft with his hands."

Russell Brandon was deft with his surveillance. He never missed a thing that happened at the casino. He could spot a card counter long before anyone else recognized the telltale signs. He had an uncanny instinct for the nature of gamblers. Russell was the first to recognize the 5'2" player with size fourteen shoes that housed a computer. Card counting was not illegal, so long as no devices were being used. The pint-size player tapped his foot along with the dealt cards, constantly checked his wrist-watch, then when the count was high, bet the table maximum. He cleaned the house. Ingenious. When management couldn't figure out what was going on, Regrettable Russell could. He had a peculiar sensibility where gamblers were concerned.

But it was the whiff of arrogance on Russell Brandon that made George Apple and the casino management dislike him. Perhaps Elle should have paid more attention to that.

CALGARY, CANADA 2016

BARRACUDA

"What can I get for you today?" Jeliane asks the woman at the coffee counter. The woman's brows are like cathedral-arches, her collagen lips reminiscent of a spring-fattened caterpillar. Her makeup is flawless, while Jeliane slapped on some Covergirl mascara prior to her early morning shift. She's wiped most of it off by now. The lineup of customers spills out of the high-end coffee shop onto the posh marble and glass wonderland of the mall. Jeliane glances at barista Matt, who is head down at the espresso machine.

She pushes her hair behind her pierced ears. She's not a redhead like her mother, but tall and blonde with the red-flushed cheeks of her Swede father. Nor is she enrolled in the art college where her parents met. Rather, she's in her first year of sociology at the university. Her mother can't figure out where she came from. Certainly not from them.

"Whose daughter *are* you?" her mother teases her.

"I'll have a medium caramel, triple shot latte. Caramel drizzle inside the cup, not on top," the woman at the coffee shop says.

"We don't have medium, only small or large." Jeliane punches the order in, writes *caramel bullshit for Kim Kardashian* on the iPad notes for Matt.

"Small or large?" Matt holds up the two sizes for the woman.

"Which is which?" she asks.

Matt rolls his eyes at Jeliane and goes back to steaming milk. Jeliane doesn't roll her green eyes, nor does she smile. Her bottom teeth are gnarly like a great barracuda. She's kicking herself for not taking her parents up on braces while she was in high school. Now she's in university and working part time at a coffee shop that charges seven bucks for a small latte and pays minimum wage.

"Did you get the caramel drizzle *inside* the cup?" the Kardashian wannabe leans over the quartz countertop.

"Got it," Jeliane snaps.

Fuck my life, she mouths at Matt. The woman and Jeliane watch Matt swirl the caramel on the sides of the cup, steam the milk, and pull the triple espresso shots. He finishes it off with a flourish of whipped cream from the silver nitrous oxide dispenser. Her drink order takes forever to make. The lineup shuffles side-to-side while they wait. Matt sets the latte down on the side counter.

"Caramel bullshit for Kim Kardas—" Matt reads from Jeliane's iPad notes, then catches himself. Jeliane howls from the till and marks the air with her finger. One for her, none for Matt.

The woman takes her latte and clicks out of the shop on her Jimmy Choos. Who wears stilettos at 8:00 a.m. before the stores are even open? The early morning walkers haven't finished their daily laps around the marble-floored mall. Likely the woman works at Nordstrom where she sells two thousand-dollar Balenciaga silk shirts while getting minimum wage. They have their salary in common.

When the next customer in line is the acne-faced guy that comes in every day, Jeliane is almost glad. He stopped at the Bank of Montreal across from the coffee shop beforehand.

"What can I get for you today?"

She avoids his name, which she knows. Russell is a regular, but she isn't *that* glad to see him. She doesn't have to look up to know that he's drilling his ocean-blue eyes into her soul.

"A ten-ounce cappuccino and a double espresso." No good morning, no hey, how are you, no happy Sunday. Weird vibe for a fifty-something-year-old guy. She knows his order by heart but makes him say it anyway. *Capp and double espresso for Fuckhead*, Jeliane writes on the iPad notes for Matt.

She glances at the floor-to-ceiling windows of the mall. Russell's white Escalade is parked in the No Parking Fire Lane with his hazard lights flashing. The rules don't apply to him. A stunning redhead who looks just like Jeliane's mother waits in the passenger seat. Jeliane watches her mother's doppelganger scroll through her cellphone. Russell stands in the corner of the shop waiting for his order.

"Think that's Russell's girlfriend?" Jeliane asks Matt. No wedding band on Russell's hands. She has no clue what Russell does for a living or why he's at the bank machine every morning. *Like, seriously, what does he do?* Not manual labour—she knows that much from his smooth hands.

"Who knows? The guy is messed. I'd be surprised if he had friends, let alone a girlfriend." Russell's taller than Matt and jacked like a former wrestler or boxer. He waits with his chin jutted out, like he's better than everyone else in the shop.

"Ten-ounce cappuccino and double espresso for fuuu—" Matt

hollers. Jeliane waits for the rest, but Matt's paying attention this time. He grins at her.

Without a word, Russell picks up his coffees and goes out into the marble/glass bliss of the mall.

"Have a nice day, Russell," Jeliane yells after him.

He doesn't glance back. He hops into his white Escalade, passes the stunning redhead her ten-ounce cappuccino, and speeds off. Jeliane shakes her head at Matt. She turns to the next customer in line.

"What can I get for you today?"

PHILIPPINES
1983

I THINK YOU SHOULD LEAVE

Bagong Silang. The telephone rang at 3:00 p.m. while the yellow sun was high in the tropical sky. Lina Santos lifted the receiver and said nothing. She listened to a man who was not her pig farmer husband. The man did not bother to identify himself. None of that mattered in this critical moment.

"It's done," he said in a low voice, like Lina knew what he meant.

"What's done?" Lina asked.

She needed the man to tell her. Other women might not need to hear it directly, but Lina was not like other women. She worked alongside her husband; they were equals. She gazed at the bundled money that Rolando had taken out and left on the kitchen counter earlier that morning. She hadn't touched it. No evidence that Rolando had had his kape at pandesal. The black coffee and bread Rolando ate every morning before he went out to feed the pigs stood untouched on the counter. Lina hadn't slept at all since the soldiers had come four nights ago, but last night, overwrought, on the cusp of something certain that she felt deep in her womb, she fell into a paralytic sleep. She'd risen and gazed out the bedroom window, catching a fleeting, last glimpse of Rolando in the passenger seat of the Mercedes. The driver was a high-ranking general whom she'd later identify in court as General Perez. He was a spokesperson for the shadow side of Marcos. It was still dark outside, and Lina held Rolando's pillow to her chest, his pig farmer musk scent embedded within. Lina tried not to cry in the black morning.

"Rolando," the man on the phone said.

Lina Santos stayed on the line, fear pulsing in her gullet until she could muster the courage to speak.

"Tell me," she said, numb and cold in the Sunday afternoon heat.

"He's dead, Lina," the man said.

With the mention of her name, Lina knew who the man was. The unusually tall soldier, the one she'd watched from their bedroom window while he smoked menthol cigarettes with Rolando in their rice field. She'd heard him say her name then, she heard him say it now. Lina was their assurance. What the exchange for the money was, Lina did not know.

"You're the tall one," Lina said. She had nothing to lose.

The man on the other end of the phone line paused.

"I think you should leave, Lina," he said, not unkindly, then hung up.

Lina listened to the dial tone, then replaced the receiver. She forced herself to walk over to the kitchen counter with the money. The pigs were squealing and restless in their pen. She hadn't let them out, hadn't fed them yet. She'd been afraid to leave the concrete house in case she missed something. A car coming down the single rutted road. With Rolando. Without Rolando. Their neighbour farmer and his plump wife perhaps, who'd been to the Sunday market in Manila. Maybe they had potential news of her husband? The mid-afternoon phone call that altered her life in ways she could not have foreseen.

She picked up the bundled money. On the bottom, there was a note that she could hardly make out in Rolando's unsteady hand. She held the note to the open window for light.

When I die. This is what you get: $50,000 PHP.

Rolando's note was simply setting their accounts straight, a chicken-scrawled note in the dead of night to inform Lina that his life, now hers, was worth $50,000 PHP. The equivalent of $1241.34 CAD. Lina knew because she had a tita *auntie* in downtown Montreal. She wanted nothing to do with any of it. She went outside and released the squealing pigs from their pen. The pigs ran ecstatically into the deep green rice field.

She folded Rolando's matter-of-fact note in her pocket—no hugs, no kisses, no expressed love, nothing but the ruthless settling of an account that in Lina's mind was not settled. She went back inside and moved through the house with purposeful fear. She packed a bag of clothing, rolled the money she and Rolando had earned honestly from the pigs they farmed. As she passed through the kitchen once more, she picked up the bundled money on the counter. She'd hide it beneath the pig's feed. She slid her bare feet into her best Sunday shoes and walked out, leaving the door of their concrete house open. On the shovel that Rolando used to clean out the pigpen, she pinned a note: Kunin mo lahat. *Take it all.*

Manila International Airport. Amado and the General had both seen the assassination, the cold-blooded murder of a pig farmer. The real assassin was on the air stairs in a Marcos uniform, not the civilian in an airport uniform murdered in broad daylight by sixteen soldiers. What Amado had really witnessed was the cunning gaze of a general who knew the outcome before the event even went down.

In the aftermath of the bloodshed, a piece of Amado expired with the shoeless pig farmer, and in turn, the man in the white safari suit. He felt like the steely-eyed general had reached deep inside his body and triggered a breaker switch. His luxury of hope was replaced by sheer terror. J-Mar and his workmates sprinted past Amado in the hangar towards the anarchy of Gate Eight. The gate that afterward, no one wanted to work.

"J-Mar don't go out there," Amado shouted from his tug cart going full throttle through the empty hangar. Amado hopped off the cart and pulled J-Mar across the hangar, leading him into the secured tunnel that ground crew used to access the runways. He shut the door. J-Mar stared at him in the dimly lit tunnel.

"Air stairsjetway the soldierrevolver themaninthewhite suit armslikeaneagle theguydressed like us," Amado said in a rapid-fire volley of words that made no sense.

Distressed, J-Mar ran his hands through his mohawk, flattening it for a few seconds before it sprung back up. Amado motioned wildly at their collective uniforms.

"Dressed like us, sixteen shots right in front of me," Amado said, the pitch of his voice rising. "The officer, oh sweet Jesus, the fucking General."

J-Mar held Amado by the shoulders to steady him. Amado breathed in and didn't exhale until the realization hit him.

"One look at the shift schedule. Gate Eight. He's got me, J-Mar," Amado said. His eyes were no longer gold, only wide black pupils.

J-Mar had no idea what he was talking about. He fumbled for a Marlboro from his breast pocket and lit it for Amado. They could still hear the shouting, the frantic bootsteps of the soldiers on the concrete floor of the hangar outside the secured door. Someone pounded on the metal door. J-Mar moved Amado further along in the tunnel away from the door.

"Tell me, my friend." J-Mar pulled Amado's quaking body into his own and after many minutes, felt Amado settle. J-Mar led him through the tunnel, and they emerged on the far side of the main terminal. Amado stared up at the blinding sun, like looking directly at a solar eclipse, or into the intense eyes of a high-ranking officer who would soon know exactly who Amado Barcelona was.

J-Mar bent down and picked up a yellow woven bracelet off the road where the roaring crowd had been. Now the crowd tried to push their way into the main terminal. J-Mar slid the yellow bracelet onto Amado's slender wrist.

"Come, my friend," J-Mar said, "we will go to my place. I don't think it's safe for you to go home." He led his friend across the acre of airport to the employee parking lot, then opened the door of his battered Corolla with a broken taillight that he'd neglected to get fixed since the last time the police had pulled him over. He helped Amado into the passenger seat like a child.

He pulled a joint from the ashtray and lit it, offering it to Amado first. Amado sucked in three successive hits, no smoke rings this time. He passed it back to J-Mar. Air-tight, overheated, J-Mar's Corolla was a literal hotbox. By the time they finished the joint at the next set of lights, neither one of them could speak. J-Mar drove too slow for the rushing Jeepneys that were brightly painted and had stolen Mercedes Benz stars affixed to the front.

"They look like circus cars," J-Mar observed.

The Jeepneys swerved recklessly around J-Mar, who drove like pulot. *Molasses*. Too slow and thick with pot for the police officer that flashed his lights and pulled up alongside signalling J-Mar to pull over. He stopped on the side of the roaring road, had the presence of mind to roll down his window, releasing the hotbox out into the moist exhaust of a million cars. The police officer got out of his cruiser, approached the passenger side first. He bent down and stared hard through the closed window at Amado. Stunned, shocked, stoned in the passenger seat, Amado stared out the cracked windshield of J-Mar's Corolla.

The officer walked around the Corolla, noted the lack of rear bumper and broken taillight. The pot was so heavy in the back of J-Mar's skull, he could not speak.

"Your brake light," Amado heard the policeman say. The policeman eyed their pale blue shirts and matching navy trousers.

"Just off work?"

"The airport." J-Mar nodded. "Just us guys in uniforms."

The officer grinned, looking for a moment like he wouldn't proceed with a ticket before changing his mind. He bent his head and filled out the ticket while J-Mar waited in stony silence.

Amado glanced sideways at the running cruiser, spotting the dead man in the back of the police car with a single bullet hole through his head. His heart thumped in his throat for the second time that day. Amado elbowed J-Mar, motioning with frantic gold eyes towards the police cruiser.

"J-Mar, look." Amado pointed to the back seat of the police cruiser.

J-Mar leaned forward in the guise of wiping the layer of dust off his dashboard. He too saw the dead man. One of Marcos's missing likely. There would be no headline in tomorrow's paper, nothing but a fraught rumour on the teeming streets of Manila about one of hundreds of dissenters that went missing. The officer looked oblivious to the dead man in the back of his cruiser. He didn't seem to care if Amado or J-Mar saw the man either. Parang wala lang. *Like it was nothing*. Just another day on the job.

The flipside of a shadow world that Amado hadn't known existed. Once he'd witnessed it, there was no going back. Only forward and away.

The police officer bent forward and handed J-Mar the ticket. Perhaps their uniforms saved them from joining the man in the back seat of the cruiser, J-Mar thought, irrationally.

"Thank you, thank you." J-Mar nodded until the police officer, satisfied or annoyed with his humility, waved his hand for them to go. J-Mar pulled out into the flow of traffic. Neither of them looked back. After a few minutes of dazed silence, J-Mar put his hand over his friend's clenched fists.

"I think you should leave, Amado," J-Mar said. "The country."

CALGARY, CANADA
1984

THIS SHELTER IS FOR YOU, LIV

In the quiet hours before the casino opened, George Apple strode across the paisley carpet and entered his office. No dealers, no tellers in the cash cage, no charity volunteers. Moose wasn't at the front security desk yet. George had the casino to himself outside of Amado Barcelona, who was on the other end of the floor vacuuming tables, clearing last night's ashtrays, and straightening leather stools. George waved across at Amado. Amado nodded and continued with his work. If George Apple had seventeen more people like Amado, his job as casino owner would be easier. As it was, he was at constant odds with unreliable dealers that failed to show up for their shifts, or worse, showed up half cocked, like Erik with his mangled tie. Still, Erik performed his blackjack duties, and the players liked him. A warm body was all that George could reasonably ask for.

He ran through the pit cards from last evening, checking the numbers against the cash cage tally. Down perhaps from their norm, but nothing drastic. He looked at the individual tables to see who the culprits were. A blackjack table was in the red and one roulette hadn't performed well. He made note of that, then gazed up and saw Amado distributing the cards in their plastic numbered shoes onto their respective blackjack tables. Shortly, the volunteers from the Sheriff King's Crisis Shelter for Women would roll in and George Apple would set them up for the next twenty-four hours. For the time being, he settled into the stack of papers on his desk, watched through his open door the casino staff rolling in.

Moose was at the security desk sipping burnt coffee from the canteen. Russell Brandon came in without Liv and walked past Moose.

He went to check in with Wayne.

"You're on table six," Wayne said. Russell strode away from the pit without any acknowledgement.

Elle walked past his table in her mid-length pink coat and long red hair. She didn't need to turn her head; she felt his gaze penetrate her. She shook him off, hung her coat in the dealers' lounge, poured a Styrofoam cup of black coffee, and then went out to the floor to check in. Amado came over while she sorted her cards.

"Where's Erik?" Elle asked, glancing around the casino.

"Not sure," Amado said. "I left him at the Holiday Inn Lounge last night. Think he stayed up late to pick up our tips."

As if on cue, Erik walked in with Liv. This was new. Liv had on large dark sunglasses that made her look like Jackie Onassis. Both Elle and Amado noticed that Liv didn't have on the thick silver dog chain she always wore around her neck. It was noticeably absent this morning, which further piqued Elle's curiosity.

"What's with that?" Elle asked.

"The sunglasses or Erik or Liv's missing dog chain?" Amado asked. He was equally observant.

"Erik."

"Maybe they are having an affair," Amado said, with a puzzling grin on his face that Elle didn't know what to make of.

Amado's gold eyes followed Erik and Liv into the breakroom like a hunter.

Erik checked in with Wayne. Erik was never talkative this early in the day; only on their drinking shifts at the Holiday Inn Lounge did Erik let loose and talk—strictly casino gossip, never personal.

"Loose lips sink ships," Amado said, so gravely that Elle stopped sorting her cards and cocked her head at him.

"What do you mean?" she asked.

Amado's private thoughts were on his loose lips, and the Marcos ships he could sink if he wasn't afraid for his life. He followed the court trials over the past year in the Philippines via the American newspapers that he purchased at a downtown newsstand. So far, there were no eyewitnesses outside of the Crying Lady from Taipei. Not credible enough to convict the sixteen soldiers or the General or to implicate the Marcos regime. Instead, the blame was placed solely on the shoeless pig farmer. Amado rubbed the yellow threaded bracelet on his wrist. His heart thudded in panic mode; he couldn't answer Elle. He was back in the moment.

When George Apple uncharacteristically stormed out of his office, Rude Rudy, The Crier, and Billy Jacked had first-class, front row seats. Wayne lagged some three feet behind in George's furious wake. George went into the dealers' lounge and led young Liv, still in her Jackie Onassis sunglasses, back into his office where he shut his door. Everyone watched with rapt interest. Wayne stood guard at the closed office door, waved his pink balloon hand at Elle and Erik to get them to sort their cards.

"Fifteen minutes until go time," Wayne mouthed at them.

Minutes later, George Apple opened the door of his office and barreled across the pit to Russell's table. At some point in their low but heated conversation, Russell stepped back from the table, undid his black apron, then threw it aggressively in Wayne's direction. The apron was not heavy enough to carry any vehemence and sailed to the floor like a flaccid parachute. It was almost comical. Moose, former NFL linebacker, was on high alert at the front desk. George Apple shook his head and called him off. The ruinous look on Russell's face made Elle flinch. She didn't need to see the mark of Russell's fist in Liv's hidden eye socket to be afraid of him. She noticed that Russell had Liv's silver dog chain around his seedy neck. What was that about? Poor Liv. George Apple marched Russell out towards the back exit.

"Don't bother coming in this week," George hollered after him.

Regrettable Russell was taller, but no match for George Apple's substantial firefighter build. He didn't give George the finger, didn't say a word; he just exited the casino. Moose went over and stood with George Apple at the exit until the fiery red on George's face was extinguished.

Elle and Amado and Erik stood at their tables. Wayne gave Liv the option of going home without pay.

"I'm sorry I can't pay you, hon bun," he said, patting Liv's exposed forearm. "Government regs. No sick pay." He looked at Liv's bare neck.

"Can I work the money wheel today, Wayne?" Liv asked. "I can't afford to miss work."

"You sure, hon bun?"

Liv nodded without speaking. Wayne changed the schedule for her. It'd be a slow day on the money wheel. The regulars were too savvy to throw their money away on the outlandish wheel odds, but Liv wandered over to the money wheel all the same, her large dark sunglasses the universal, shameful code for battered females.

Not long after, the same trio of the young white male, Filipino mother, and her son in dark Ray-Bans floated past the blackjack tables. Amado nodded at them.

"Labing-anim," Amado said in Tagalog. Not the same good morning greeting as yesterday, Elle noted. The sunglassed player nodded back, while the mother and white male proceeded to take over the blackjack table next to Erik's.

Rude Rudy sat down at Elle's table, which was almost full. An elderly gentleman with a hearing aid was in the anchor spot. Elle hoped to some God that this man knew what he was doing. She fanned her cards across the green felt, then shuffled.

"How's it going today?" she asked Rudy.

"Oh, it*'s going*," Rudy said. He was such a drama king. They both laughed.

He laid out several brown hundred-dollar bills.

He was a stockbroker by day, but from his regular attendance at the casino, Elle wondered when Rudy had time to do anything else. She enjoyed his company at her blackjack table right up until the moment he lost the contents of his wallet and then lost his V-chip. It was early in the day yet, with plenty of time for reasonable conversation—an extraordinary commodity among players.

"Is she okay?" Rudy asked, glancing over at Liv in her large dark sunglasses on the money wheel.

"I don't know," Elle said. "You should do her a favour and ask her yourself."

"Maybe later."

Rudy put his hands together in mock prayer.

"Be nice to me today, Elle?" he asked.

"Then don't play at my table, Rudy. Go home. Take your mother out for lunch. Buy your girlfriend a cashmere sweater." Elle didn't know why she bothered. She didn't even know if Rudy had a girlfriend or a mother. Rudy never took her seriously. Regardless, she liked the duplicity of Rudy. He was witty and acerbic, his intelligence well above the rest of the generic players.

Elle offered the red cut card to Rudy, who sliced the cards like he was wielding a samurai sword. The other players murmured their appreciation for Rudy's opening gambit. It was a complex game that required all their mad skills. Then Elle dealt the cards as fast as she could, scarcely giving the players a chance to pause in the first two shoes. Weed them out early, then only the diehard players would stick around. The elderly gentlemen on anchor with hearing aids in both ears doubled down and split his tens. His split tens resulted in Elle pulling a blackjack. The table recoiled. Elle heard Rudy react under his breath. She shook her head at Rudy, but he kept his head down, wouldn't engage.

Three shoes later, despite the negative returns the first time around, the hard-of-hearing man split his tens again and lost. The table erupted. Rudy pulled more hundred-dollar bills from his wallet and slammed them down on the table. The elderly man grew weary of the table's dissent, took his hearing aids out and played in blissful silence. Rudy looked desperately around for another table to escape to, but the casino was humming, going full bore. There was nowhere else to go.

The trio of regulars played at the blackjack table next to Erik's. Wayne was glued to the table, which meant that the table was losing. The dealer was obviously dumping his chip tray to the high rolling players. If it got serious enough, George Apple would appear shortly. Wayne hoped to avoid that. The young Filipino in his dark sunglasses sat on the anchor. Elle wondered why he wore sunglasses. Stoned, hungover, or a criminal, perhaps? The volunteers from the Sheriff King's Crisis Shelter looked as worried as Wayne did about their potential losses.

On Elle's table with the heedless anchor, Rudy held on for as long as he could. But then the elderly man hit his sixteen against Elle's three. The man broke and Elle made her hand.

"*Jesusfuckingchristalmightyfuckingcunt*" Rudy erupted. The hard-of-hearing man heard nothing. The other players stopped complaining in the bombastic light of Rude Rudy.

Elle scooped up the cards and chips.

"You can't call people cunts."

Rudy looked at her with a mercurial face. Elle knew he was at his breaking point.

"Fuck off," Rudy said.

Elle straightened up. She tried. She might not have mustered the courage to leave her deadbeat boyfriend, but she wasn't taking any guff from Rude Rudy, no matter how much she liked his sardonic, wise-cracking demeanour.

"Pit boss!" Elle hollered.

Wayne detached himself from the trio's table and came over. Elle tilted her head in Rudy's direction.

"Deal him out for a couple hands, sweetie," Wayne said.

No need for Elle to waste time explaining what Rudy had done this time.

Wayne reached over and patted the green felt in front of Rudy.

"Simmer down there, Big Rig," he said, like he was Rudy's grandfather.

Rudy's rig was small and tight and compact but in the presence of a conciliatory eighty-year-old man, Rudy could hardly argue.

Rudy signalled for a marker, then stomped off towards the canteen for a cup of coffee. When he returned, he wouldn't make eye contact with Elle. Elle felt a stab of remorse. She didn't like taking anyone's money, even if it was for the women's emergency shelter. The elderly man on anchor was under siege from the rest of the table, like rabid seagulls on a yacht lunch. Rudy picked up his remaining chips, pushed back his marker, and to Elle's surprise, headed for the money wheel.

In his open office, George Apple looked up from his paperwork and sprawl of pit cards. Always one blackjack table in arrears these days, it seemed. Never the same table, of course. That'd be too easy. Not the same dealer. No rhyme or reason to it, but he knew something was off. He sighed. Out on the floor, Rude Rudy pulled the last hundred-dollar bill from his wallet and laid it down on the money wheel. Liv broke the bill down into twenty-five-dollar chips, the wheel maximum. Rudy plunked a black chip down on the Joker. The bet was no joke with odds of forty-five to one. Rudy wasn't a diplomatic loser, but he was also no reckless player. Neither George nor Elle took their eyes off him. George, concerned for Liv, got up from his office chair and wandered over. He stood beside the money wheel within reach of Liv.

"Are you okay, Liv?" Rudy asked.

Liv in her dark sunglasses, sans her silver dog chain, screwed up her face for a moment like she might cry. Rudy waited for her to regain herself.

"Spin it, Liv," Rudy said.

Liv spun the money wheel as hard as she could. The wheel *ticked ticked ticked* until it came to a stop on one of the plentiful dollar bills. She watched Rudy as she picked up his twenty-five-dollar chip. Rudy banged down another. George side-eyed him. Rudy picked it up and laid it down gently this time.

"Spin it, Liv."

Liv spun. She picked up his losing chip. He bet the Joker twice more. Liv scooped his chip up with shaking hands. She couldn't take any more male violence today. When he lost the last of his hundred-dollar bill, Rudy pulled out his blackjack chips from Elle's table. He set down the eighty plus chips in front of Liv.

"Buy yourself a cashmere sweater, Liv," he said, though he knew she wouldn't personally get it. Tips were shared with the rest of the dealers.

Liv's chin weakened, then she put her head down and cried beneath her sunglasses. One of the Sheriff King Shelter volunteers, recognizing the telltale signs of a sunglassed woman in trouble, came over in solidarity. She rubbed Liv's back while she cried. George Apple stepped in, thanking Rude Rudy for the generous tip. Rudy walked out of the casino without looking back. Elle watched, amazed, vindicated in her affection for Rudy despite his gambler shortcomings.

"Got someplace safe to go, Liv?" George asked.

The Sheriff King woman handed Liv a pocket packet of Kleenex.

"My mother's." Liv removed her sunglasses to wipe her face. Elle winced at the sight of Liv's blackened eye. Liv put her hand to her bare neck. Was Liv free now? Was the necklace a souvenir for Russell to remember her by?

George's face hardened at the sight of Liv's black eye. Russell wouldn't be coming back next week nor the week after. He wouldn't be coming back at all.

"Need cab fare?" he asked.

Liv nodded. George pulled out his wallet and gave Liv everything he had.

CALGARY, CANADA
2016

VARSITY ACRES

Through her Varsity Acres basement window, Jeliane spots the ex-husband that lives in a teardrop trailer. He and his ex-wife upstairs must have purchased the small trailer prior to having three shrieking children. The ex-husband crosses the backyard that's littered with a Little Tyke's slide, a Cook with Me kitchenette, and a petroleum plastic Barbie palace that won't disintegrate within Jeliane's lifetime. The ex-husband steps through the toy minefield financed by his alimony payments back when he had a job.

The man knocks softly on the upstairs door.

"Could I use the shower?" he whisper-asks through the wood door.

"Not now, I'm busy bathing your children." The reply comes from his harassed wife. Clearly, they can't afford to live apart. The man retreats to his Sad Dad trailer. Jeliane glances at the corner of the yard to a second-hand BBQ her Swede father gave her when she moved in. The propane tank she just filled up is gone.

It's her birthday today and she wants to have her friends over for a wiener roast. She used the last of this month's student loan to fill the tank.

Jeliane pulls on her yoga pants and marches out to the backyard to find the tank. She looks under the slide, opens the pink petroleum doors of the Barbie palace, then spies her newly filled propane tank attached to Sad Dad's trailer.

How can she ask for it back? The guy has no job, no wife, no shower, and three kids that barely speak to him. Is she going to be the last nail in this guy's coffin?

She snaps a pic of the propane tank attached to the trailer and sends it to her Snapchat group. *No wienies for my birthday. Sad face*. Seven lightning fast sad, mad faces appear shortly after, which make her feel glad.

She goes back inside. The ex-wife controls the thermostat upstairs. It's Antarctica in her basement suite. A warm text from her mother comes in: *Happy birthday Jellybean!! Dinner tonight? YASSS*, she texts back. She has half a carton of almond milk in the fridge, a pack of wieners, and eight hotdog buns. Outside her basement window, Sad Dad lights a joint. He's roasting a smokie on his propane fire pit. No shower today and no reason to even try. High on pot and her propane fumes before it's even noon. She snaps a pic of Sad Dad and sends it to her group chat. *I'm not even laughing on my birthday*. Matt from the coffee shop texts back *HAPPY BIRTHDAY JEL, buy you a hotdog at work. Heart, heart.*

In her bathroom, Jeliane strips down and showers until the hot water tank runs out, which barely gives her time to shampoo and rinse her white blonde hair. She'll shave her legs next time. She spends the rest of the afternoon curled in the plaid fuzzy Costco blanket her mother bought, studying for her Second Wave Feminist test tomorrow at 8:00 a.m. Who schedules SWF exams at that time in the morning?

Three hours later, Jeliane opens her eyes. The SWF book she's reading is on the same page. She might be more exhausted than she realizes. Now she'll have to study after dinner. The pressure of five sociology courses, four days a week at the mall, and amassing student debt that by the time her four-year degree is done will add up to sixty thousand dollars, is overwhelming. The thought of the debt alone makes her head throb. She doesn't have rich parents.

When her parents knock at her basement door, they have a birthday card in hand. Her father smiles. Jeliane beams, showing her gnarly teeth. Inside the card is the gift of reality star teeth. Invisalign braces. No more barracuda. She might live to smile again. Her mother pulls her into a bear hug. They go out to Swiss Chalet for chicken dinner, winner, winner.

MANILA, PHILIPPINES
1983

SNAPSHOT OF A REVOLUTION

Aurora Aquino spotted Ken Kashiwahara and the other journalists through the glass in the main lobby. Ken's head was buried in his hands.

"Ken! Ken!" she shouted.

The young soldier held her back.

Ken rushed towards her, and because of his media badge, was permitted to leave. Everyone else in the airport was not. No one left, no one entered. Ken embraced Aquino's tiny mother in his arms.

"Ninoy?" she asked, and stared up at him with hard, dry eyes. They were the eyes of a mother that already knew too many political sacrifices. Her husband first, surely not her son too?

"There were shots. We couldn't see. We don't know yet." Ken knew the danger in substantiating unconfirmed facts.

"They've taken him to the hospital, I think," Ken said, though he knew. Everyone on the plane that day knew.

Soon after, Aquino's wife Corazon and their five children in New York would get a call. The oldest daughter answered the phone.

"Is it true that your father has been killed in the Manila International Airport?" the correspondent asked. "Can you confirm?"

A shockwave moved across Aquino's daughter's face; her mother Corazon seized the phone and struggled to maintain a semblance of parental calm until they knew for certain. Her roiling stomach said otherwise. Then other news outlets called—UPI and AP. It wasn't until their friend, Japanese Congressman Shintaro Ishihara, called from Tokyo and verified the shooting, that they knew too. In fact, the whole world outside the Philippines knew what Ninoy's mother didn't. Media across the entire country was blacked out by Ferdinand and Imelda Marcos, fearful that if the Filipino people knew what had happened, they might storm Malacañang Palace.

With Ken's small, fierce mother-in-law in his arms, his restraint gave out. He gave into the shock and exhaustion, his russet eyes filling. Aurora Aquino remained stoic. She prayed wordlessly to the Blessed Mother that everyone was wrong, her son Ninoy in the same white safari suit that he'd left the country in three years ago would waltz through the airport doors and fold her in his arms.

Even though it was confirmed an hour later via a French radio station, Aurora Aquino did not know, and even when she did, she would not cry for a full day over the death of her son. No record of what had happened at the Manila International Airport was released anywhere in the country until the on-board journalists released their sun-blinded videos and hurriedly developed photographs back to the US, Canada, France, Taipei, and Japan. The whole world saw the overexposed black and white images, the unclear, grainy videos of the two bodies laid out on the runway before Aquino's mother even shed a single tear.

The following Monday, Ken walked the early morning streets to clear his head. He saw panicked people pounding on bank doors, demanding to withdraw their money. The Filipino people stormed the grocery stores and came out with overflowing carts, then hurried home to barricade themselves for whatever would come next. The lack of news coupled with the multiplying rumours had instilled a new kind of terror in them. Surely the full force of Marcos's militarized government would rain down on them.

Ken collapsed down on a nearby park bench. He watched the security guard throw open the gilded bank doors. He let the people make their way inside unimpeded and then stood on the marble steps of the bank. He pulled out his tumpong and in the frenzy of the hysterical mob, he played Bayan Ko, *My Homeland*. A fluted song of defiance. The people paused and then applauded the bank guard. For all they knew, he could be Marcos's next missing person tomorrow; like a deadly game of Bingo, his number might be called—but not today. Today, the bank guard was the brazen Filipino hero they needed.

Ken Kashiwahara knew from journalistic experience that there were things you could not capture in a photograph or convey in a news article. You had to be there to feel it deep in your breastbone. The guard's bamboo flute seared Ken's grief and in the span of the defiant, hopeful song, made it whole again. Ken put his head in his hands for the second time in two days and cried for his brother-in-law. Ninoy might have lived a hundred years, but he could never accomplish what his death would. He wished Ninoy were here to see it—to feel the wounded, inflamed heart of Manila that his demise had ignited.

It was half an hour before Ken could muster the wherewithal

to make his way back to Times Street where Ninoy's mother had laid her son's body in state until Corazon and their five children returned from the US. Both mother and widow insisted on the same white safari suit stained black with Ninoy's spilled blood; no funeral makeup would be applied over his cut and bruised face, and the casket would be laid wide open for the world to see, even if the media was still dark in the country.

In the hours following the run on the banks and the emptied grocery stores, people emerged from their houses and made their way to Times Street. The August monsoon cried down on them. Women and men had yellow ribbons tied around the foreheads, attached to their wrists, in bows on their children's arms; the yellow ribbons were intended for Ninoy's welcome home, but soon it would mean something else entirely. A united rebellious cry.

People lined the streets and raised their umbrellas against the monsoon.

"Put your umbrellas down," a young man in the crowd yelled through a megaphone. "Only Imelda Marcos uses umbrellas."

People laid their umbrellas down in the wet streets and left them there. An impromptu art happening, a pretty revolution in the making, thousands of multi-coloured umbrellas were splayed open and vulnerable on the weeping streets of Manila.

Ninoy's mother, more than anyone, knew the crowds risked the military wrath of Marcos. They risked their very lives to see if the rumours were true. No media dared tell them otherwise. The people waited patiently, their lines snaking up and down both sides of Times Street to see for themselves what the Marcoses had done to Aurora Aquino's son. Aurora opened the door of Ninoy's house and sat in the dining room adjacent to his bloodied, bruised body. She watched people enter the house at the rate of forty, fifty a minute. Their quiet respect was accompanied by silver and gold crosses hung around their necks.

They kissed their tiny crosses and pressed them against Ninoy's bruised forehead. What had died with him on the tarmac now gave birth to something else on Times Street. Was it the six stages of grief or the beginning of a revolution? Numbness. Shock. Hurt. Bitterness. Outrage. Anger. Aurora and the crowds saw themselves as gentle people, not prone to assassination, not prepared to accept murder in the bright yellow of a Sunday afternoon.

"My boy," she said. Then she put her head down, and despite the presence of strangers, cried for her dead son.

Her son was lying in state for days. Corazon and the children had not yet arrived from the US. The daring crowds of Filipinos increased to a point that his mother had to move Ninoy's body to Sto. Domingo, the nearby church.

Early that morning, a line of taxi drivers waited outside the church.

"Why are you here so early?" Aquino's mother asked them.

"We have to report to work at 6:00 a.m.," they told her. "This is the only time we could come."

Aurora touched her fractured heart; the shy drivers averted their eyes. After the taxi drivers left, the women with big wicker baskets came. Fish vendors from the market that opened at 8:00 a.m. The only time the women could come. In the church itself, old men and women lay down on the hardwood pews and slept, waiting their turn. In the afternoon, the Zobels, a prominent family; and the Makati businessmen; secretaries; and the Jeepney-riding proles came. Rolando's neighbour had been to the Manila market the previous Sunday when Senator Aquino was assassinated. The farmer returned home and saw Rolando's pigs wandering his rice field.

"Far too late to be out," he commented to his plump wife.

"Rolando must be away," the wife said. She watched the foraging pigs.

The farmer walked the length of the ylang-ylang trees and stopped in at the concrete house to check on Lina. No sign of her or Rolando. There was an odd note on the shovel that he failed to understand. Kunin mo lahat. *Take it all.*

He gathered the pigs into their pen for the night. He found the bundled money beneath the bag of feed for the pigs. He'd leave the money there until the rumours of Rolando Galman's death were substantiated. The first thing the media released was that Rolando had been a hitman for a communist rebel group.

For a month, the neighbouring farmer looked after the pigs and tended the rice field. His wife picked the fragrant yellow blooms of the ylang-ylang and took them to the Sunday market to sell for Lina if she came back to their concrete house. She didn't. Only then did the farmer and his wife take the bundled money and distribute it evenly among the other families in the community. Exactly what Rolando Galman would have done. No one in the community believed the reports and they questioned the court trial where they posthumously convicted Rolando Galman based on the testimony of sixteen eyewitness soldiers. This had Marcos written all over it and the entire country smelled the pig rot corruption pungent in their farmer nostrils.

In Sto. Domingo, the pig farmer and his plump wife stood in their rubber shoes. The poor and the rich waited side by side in the reverential hush of the stone church. They, along with thousands of Filipinos, paid their respects to Ninoy.

The masses rose from thousands into two million for Ninoy's funeral procession. Mahatma Gandhi's funeral had produced a million mourners. If only Corazon had allowed the funeral procession to proceed past Malacañang Palace that day, two-million Filipinos might have toppled the Marcos regime then and there. But she didn't.

"There is a time to grieve and a time to rise," she said after she'd decided not to pass by the palace. "This is not the time to rise."

The potent power of dead leaders, Ken wrote in his notebook. Benigno Aquino Jr.'s death trick. He saw the transformation on the faces of the mourners, their distress—their sad laments replaced by something else. Anger. He felt it too, as if he'd been orphaned like the rest of the country. No longer was it enough to simply observe and report as a journalist; it was time to pick a side and serve.

Amado Barcelona didn't come. He slipped south to Davao City. Far easier to leave the locked-down country from there. Away from prying eyes, he flew out of Malaysia and then to English-speaking Canada, a place with a language he was fluent in.

"One-way ticket to Canada," he told the airport agent.

"Where in Canada?" the ticket agent asked. Amado Barcelona looked wildly around the airport until he spotted the poster on the wall.

"Calgary, Canada." He had no one anywhere but here in his homeland—the destination did not matter. All that mattered was away. Safely out of the lethal reach of General Perez, who had indeed pulled the Manila airport records and singled him out. Amado Barcelona, the baggage handler in the tug cart, the man with gold eyes who'd witnessed political assassination and cold-blooded murder in one fell swoop. The man who knew what the General knew.

In Sto. Domingo church, Lina Santos gazed down into the bruised, gentle face of the man her husband had assassinated. What had Rolando done to their hope? To their country's last hope for democracy? She didn't believe it. She couldn't. She pressed her small gold cross onto the stained chest of Ninoy's safari suit, then brought her lips to the cross to taste his familial blood. As Lina Santos turned to leave, she bumped into a man behind her dressed in an airport uniform and with his hair in a black, shining mohawk.

CALGARY, CANADA 1984

SORRY ABOUT THE CARPET

The moon was absent in late August when Amado led Erik down the cedar steps to the basement suite that he rented in a luxury home. It was for sale for one Canadian dollar—a way for his distraught landlord to avoid the bank's liabilities. It was the bright days and black nights of 1984 when Calgarians were in the red with housing foreclosures and bankruptcies. When Oil boomed. When Oil bust. Pipelines were halted, American conglomerates fled south. People in South Calgary, fraught with despair and freefalling debt, jumped out the windows of their defunct Oil and Gas office towers. Nurses and cabbies, teachers and meatpackers, marched together in strike camaraderie. The city was a barely thriving mess.

Amado's neighbours sold their over-leveraged home for cheap with its contents included, as if they dropped everything they'd been doing and walked out of their custom wood doors imported from Spain. Half-eaten eggs Florentine sat on the teak dining room table while a roaring-new Jaguar languished in the three-car garage. Highly leveraged like everything else. Corvettes, Porsches, and Mercedes Benzes for bargain basement prices everywhere. A dystopian oil fiction played out on the real streets of bleak Calgary.

Amado eased drunk Erik gently onto his futon. Erik covered his face with his hands.

"Don't look at me, Amado," Erik said, briefly aware that this might not be his finest hour. His dark hair was loose, not styled in his usual impeccable coif.

At midnight, Erik blacked out and went quiet. Amado stood on his *Millennium Falcon* carpet; he missed his baggage buddy J-Mar, he missed the tropical monsoons, he missed his one-room apartment in Manila surrounded by six million Filipino brothers and sisters where he was never alone.

He stripped off Erik's black shoes and ankle socks; the sight of Erik's naked feet made him want to weep. For a Jesus moment, he held Erik's vulnerable feet in his warm hands. Then he tucked Erik in from head to foot with the Hermes cashmere blanket his landlord had given him.

Amado pulled the blanket up under Erik's chin. Amado spared Erik from another uncomfortable night in his Impala. Too drunk to drive, too drunk to retrieve everyone's tips, but drunk enough to spend the night in his Chevy Impala in the Holiday Inn parking lot without minding. There was nothing Amado could do about that. The scope of Oil was so outside his paltry casino job that he couldn't see the fuss, didn't understand the grave calamity.

Amado left Erik to sleep it off and retired to his single bed in the other room. He smoked a Marlboro in the dark, his time when he replayed the black tarmac movie in his head. Starting with the blood-stained man in the white safari suit, then onto the shoeless pig farmer, wrongly accused, posthumously convicted.

Double indignity. Ending with the deadly eyes of the high-ranking military officer that constricted his throat. General Perez was synonymous with the shadow side of the Marcos government. If the General's morose face appeared on the front page of the Manila newspaper, it meant another missing person. Amado felt guilt for not staying, and then for not going back later to testify. He could have collaborated with the Crying Lady's testimony. He followed Marcos's stacked court trial that played out in the US newspapers. Alternate evidence versus the plausibility of what really happened. So many conflicting testimonies, blurred photographs, and conspiracy theories corroborated by sun-blinded videos.

Amado thought in the dark; if someone like Senator Aquino had no guarantee of a safe return to his homeland, what assurances did a lone baggage handler have? None that Amado saw. He smoked Marlboros until his lungs ached.

At some point in the night, he heard Erik retching in the other room. At some point when the August sun broached the horizon, Amado fell into an exhausted sleep. When he woke, he peered in the other room at Erik who was still asleep on the futon. A dark stain like spilled blood was spread on his Millennium Falcon carpet. Amado caught his breath. He couldn't deal with that.

Erik sensed his presence and opened his eyes.

"Amado?" he asked cautiously, not sure if he'd overstayed his welcome. It happened a lot. Erik's had a sea of exes. One ex in the Netherlands obliged him to pay child support; after a decade of silence, his thirteen-year-old son sent him a picture. Erik saw the uncanny resemblance, a shiny, hope-filled pubescent version of himself. The boy had dark glimmering eyes and thick black hair impeccably styled like Erik's. The sheer optimism on the boy's face gave Erik pause. This boy had a choice, a chance. Erik began wiring money to his ex. The reason he gave Elle the stop sign hand whenever she interrogated him at the lounge was that he couldn't talk about his abandoned boy without his Dutch heart breaking.

"Did I touch you?" Erik looked at Amado in the bedroom doorway.

Amado didn't answer.

Erik sat up and massaged his throbbing head, then glanced down at the Millennium Falcon carpet that he hadn't noticed last night. He saw the dark stain of his Black Russian vomit.

"Oh god," Erik said, burying his handsome face in his hands.

The price of friendship, Amado thought. He knew the price of loneliness.

"That's okay, my friend, it happens to the best of us. I'll see you at work."

Worn-out from the late night at the Holiday Inn Lounge and the rest of his horror-filled night, Amado stopped in the morning at the downtown newsstand for a coffee and a newspaper. The World News headline in the *Calgary Herald*: "Filipinos Mark One Year Anniversary of Aquino Murder." The accompanying photograph showed half a million people, a sea of yellow-wrapped fists pumping the Manila air of their homeland. He twisted the yellow threaded bracelet on his wrist, climbed back into his car and drove to the casino. Every time he glanced down at the photograph, he had to fight back tears, lash his solitude to the nearest available person. At that moment, Erik.

After Amado left for work, Erik showered and in his search for a clean shirt, flipped through the neat pile of international money orders on Amado's dresser. Who was Jejomar? A letter read: "Don't Come Back." A scorned ex? Maybe Amado had left a child behind in the Philippines too? Erik pulled some wadded-up twenties that he hadn't spent at the Holiday Inn

Lounge and added them to the pile of receipts. The least he could do in exchange for Amado wrestling him from the Holiday Inn Lounge and sparing him a restless night in his Impala.

When he got to work, Erik strode across the paisley carpet to Amado who was just finishing up distributing the numbered card shoes onto their respective numbered tables. He knew Amado missed the Philippines like he missed being his son's father. Amado clutched the *Calgary Herald* in one hand and smoked a Marlboro in the other. Erik reached out and put his hand on Amado's tense shoulders.

"Sorry about the carpet," Erik said, his eyes welling.

MANILA, PHILIPPINES
1984

UNTIL LAMBS BECOME LIONS

On the one-year anniversary of Aquino's assassination, the inflamed hearts of the Filipino people were ablaze. Lina Santos hurried along the empty streets in Metro Manila. Mid-Wednesday, the streets were normally bustling with rushing cars and Jeepneys, people and bicycles and goats galore. Her thin yellow t-shirt clung to her skin. The vacant street made her feel extra vulnerable. She alone could identify General Perez as the high-ranking officer who had retrieved her husband Rolando Galman exactly one year ago. She knew at least six persons connected with the Senator's assassination who had either been killed or were reported missing. She didn't know which was worse: dead and sorted out, or alive and in constant terror of being killed. Rolando's sister was still MIA a year after the fact. The communal chatter was rampant about the ongoing trial. Who to believe? Who to discredit? There'd been talk of a baggage handler who'd also gone missing who might have witnessed the assassination and murder on the runway.

She was grateful that no one outside AWAR, the Alliance of Women Towards Action and Reconciliation, knew who she was. And even they didn't know she was the *missing* wife of the pig farmer cum communist hitman. If she'd known that the baggage handler was not one of Marcos's missing in the Philippines, but that he was a blackjack dealer living in English-speaking Canada, she'd have found a bizarre solace in Amado Barcelona's nightmares. She'd have watched Rolando smoking Hope Luxuries on the black tarmac. She'd have known that the Magnum .57 was still in his trouser pocket and that he'd not drawn the gun or fired a shot. She'd witness her conflicted husband talking and laughing as the first shot rang out on the air stairs.

Then, in those fatal seconds afterwards, she'd witness the soldiers who'd smoked and laughed with her husband raise their handguns and fire sixteen shots directly into Rolando's chest, wiping the fraught smile from his face.

In the months after Rolando's death, Lina's bloodied fetus was aborted into the cracked porcelain of a shared toilet down the hall from her studio apartment in Manila. Unceremoniously swift, Lina had no time to mark the double tragedy. After the cramps released her, she lay down on the concrete floor beside the filthy bathtub, her body curled in the same position as the terminated fetus. She cried until she couldn't anymore. No husband, no child. No keepsake of her beloved Rolando. No place to bury her grief. No body to bury her disgraced husband.

She rose and wiped the blood from her shuddering thighs. She wouldn't risk infection by using the filthy bathtub. She flushed the toilet and watched as the tiny fetus, her Hope Luxury, swirled down the bowl. She pressed her gold cross to her trembling lips and prayed for better days ahead.

On the empty street in broad daylight, Lina prayed that no one recognized her. She rounded the corner to Mendiola Street and saw the lines of a dozen organizations readied like a parade. She recognized the lead group, the League of Filipino Students. Plucky, fearless young women and men were linked arm-in-arm so they wouldn't be separated. Behind them was the Philippine Democratic Party, and then the PDP-Laban, and the MFP Movement for a Free Philippine. And behind that, her own group of AWAR women waited. She rushed towards them in open relief.

"L.K.!" the women greeted her. No one used their real names for fear of retribution, especially Lina, who was a known, much sought-after quantity by the General.

Lina flashed an "L" with her right hand, not to be confused with the loser sign that Americans sometimes flashed on television programs. Lina's was the Filipino symbol for Laban. *Fight.*

She took her place among the women. Up the street, the perimeter of the Malacañang Palace was surrounded by rolled barbed wire. No line of colourful Jeepneys or snaking line of tourists waited to visit the luxurious palace. There was no doubt in Lina's mind that their peaceful march was viewed as a threat, and a direct siege on the Marcoses. None carried weapons or donned gas masks, and outside the 86-year-old Senator on the front line who wore a yellow helmet, everyone else, including Lina, was bare-headed and barehanded. Their only means of aggression were their yellow t-shirts and the ten-foot-high bronze statue of Senator Benigno Aquino that the US had gifted them. A row of young men carried the statue on their shoulders at the back.

Their common interest: to oust Marcos and restore democracy in their homeland. Aquino's assassination had ignited that flame. Lina had no doubt that Imelda and Ferdinand were under heavy guard and cowering inside the gilded palace. Fire trucks equipped with water cannons barricaded the street on the other end. Uniformed police backed by armed troops lined both sides of the street near the palace.

The line of students lurched forward. Chanting and singing, they were followed by Lina and her women, mothers and teenagers, nuns and priests, businessmen and rice farmers, doctors and fishmongers and taxi drivers alike. There was a rare thread between the working poor and the professional class—Lina felt their camaraderie deep in her pelvis. The yellow-clad crowd sang Bayan Ko, *My Homeland*, as they neared the palace. In response, the soldiers bent down and picked up rocks covered in newspaper and lobbed them into the peaceful crowd. Lina shielded her head with her arms and pushed forward with her sisters. She'd do this for Rolando. She'd do this for her country. She'd do this for herself. All around her, bloodied people dispersed and sought refuge beneath the shelter of the kalumpit and pahtuna trees on the boulevard.

When the rocks didn't deter the crowd, the fire trucks unleashed their water cannons. Then the line of police and soldiers armed with .38s and .45s, riot shields, helmets and protective masks advanced on the crowd. Lina felt her stomach drop. *Run and find shelter,* her rational mind screamed. But her irrational mind told her that this was everyone's Laban. *Fight.* Lina investigated the haughty faces of the soldiers on either side of the street. It was easy to have courage when you were armed to the hilt. She had nothing on but her thin yellow t-shirt.

The soldiers launched silver canisters into their midst. They landed with a distinct *clank* on the pavement, dispersing tear gas which wafted over them. Lina covered her face with a lemon-soaked cloth and kept her head high. The tear gas was low to the ground. She turned and gave the sizable man behind her an extra handkerchief also soaked in lemon. She didn't know where her courage came from—maybe the fear itself, maybe her year in hiding, maybe the frontline students, maybe the yellow-helmeted senator, maybe the nuns dressed in pink habits. She didn't know which, but she was glad for it.

Then the audacious *pop pop pop* of rifles fired directly into the crowd. The soldier's guns bellowed loud and clear.

"Run!" the senator at the front yelled.

One thousand people scattered. The large man behind overtook Lina in the bedlam. A bullet caught him in the back. The bullet that would have been hers, not his. He fell in front of Lina and dropped her handkerchief. Four men picked him up and before they dragged him off to the nearest apartment, Lina stuffed the handkerchief into his shirt pocket. She wanted him to remember Filipino decency. Not Filipinos that shot into the crowd of their fellow brothers and sisters. She could scarcely believe it, even though she'd witnessed it firsthand. Lina ran until her legs and lungs were on fire. Then she ran more. She heard the popcorn pop of pistols, the singing rifle bullets. When she glanced sideways, she recognized the terrorized faces of those she ran past.

She sprinted the three kilometres to Rizal Park, where half a million people stood in camaraderie. Not the two million people on this same day a year ago who'd come out for Aquino's funeral march—the only thing that had kept her from putting her head in their gas oven. There was safety in the five hundred thousand people that were crammed into Rizal Park. The crowd lit up and roared when Lina and their thousand poured into the park. The men carrying the ten-foot bronze statue lifted a smiling Ninoy high up into the air. Like he alone, despite no longer being among the living, would save them.

When Lina caught her breath, when her throat released, when the clank of tear gas canisters and the bellows of guns ceased in her head, only then did she raise her head and look around.

The atmosphere here in Rizal Park was so different from Mendiola Street. Almost like a festival. Here, the street hawkers sold yellow t-shirts and wide banners that read "OUST MARCOS." Grinning posters of Ninoy Aquino made her heart ache. To her, Ninoy's smiling face was synonymous with Rolando's guilty face that was plastered on the front of every newspaper.

Beaming children and their parents were perched on top of the meridian in the middle of the eight-lane highway. The mood in the park was high and infectious.

On the highway, she witnessed a businessman pull over in his shiny silver Audi. He got out, unbuttoned his white-collared shirt and pulled on a yellow t-shirt instead. *Like Superman*, Lina thought. A businessman one minute, a hero the next. The crowds on the meridian cheered in approval. In the park, men and women, students and workers, scaled the power poles to see the speaker on the stage.

A tiny woman at the front of Rizal Park was dressed entirely in yellow.

"Sit down my friends, so everyone at the back can see," Corazon Aquino instructed the crowd. Not Ninoy's mother this time, but his still-grieving wife. She would not stop grieving for a full five years.

"A day to mark death. Your leader. My husband. A day to mark change. A day to mark restored democracy," Corazon Aquino called.

Close to the front, Lina spotted sixteen men dressed in pale blue shirts and navy trousers. No shoes on their naked feet. The same uniform the soldiers had delivered to Rolando. Her heart stuttered. The same uniform she'd seen on her dead husband on the front pages of countless newspapers. His pale blue shirt was marred by sixteen bullet holes.

Cardboard signs were strung around their necks that read: "FALL GUY" in English, no doubt for the benefit of the foreign journalists present. The Japanese journalist who had covered Aquino's assassination last year was interviewing the man with the jet-black mohawk that she'd inadvertently run into at Sto. Domingo church at Ninoy Aquino's wake. She waited until the journalist was done, then approached the mohawk man. Something in her still-open wound told her that he could help. The same way she knew she could help Corazon Aquino when the time was right.

"Ninoy Aquino," Corazon bellowed, louder than metal canisters, louder than guns. With half a million others, Lina Santos raised her hand and joined the sea of yellow-wrapped fists. A journalist hidden deep in the crowd had a red maple leaf on his media pass. The Canadian journalist raised his 35mm camera high above the crowd and snapped photograph after photograph after photograph that would appear eleven thousand, one hundred and thirty-eight kilometers away in the World News section of the *Calgary Herald* the next morning.

CALGARY, CANADA
2016

HOW NOT TO BE

Before the early morning mall walkers hit the quartz countertop of the coffee shop, Jeliane and Matt watch Russell at the bank machine. The redhead, her mother's doppelganger, sits outside in the white Cadillac Escalade in the fire lane. The redhead checks her makeup in the visor mirror then scrolls through her phone. Russell retrieves the wad of bills from the bank machine and stuffs them inside his vintage leather jacket.

"Sucked about your birthday BBQ last week," Matt says.

"Trailer guy must be desperate."

Matt leans down, pulls on his vape, and exhales the white cloud beneath the counter while Jeliane cleans the espresso machine.

"I'm going to steal my propane tank back," Jeliane says, refilling the sleeves and cups.

"*Dude*. What do you think a forty-year-old guy who lives in a trailer, has no job, no wife, no life, is going to do?" Matt crooks his brow at her.

"*Dude*, it's mine."

Russell strides across the marble floor towards them.

"You'll be his first murder victim. Leave him, Jel. He's got enough shit on his plate. I'll buy you a hotdog today."

"He's too stoned to murder people." Jeliane pushes the tip jar at Russell when he steps up to the counter.

Matt nods at him. Russell nods back.

"Who's too stoned to murder people?" Russell asks Matt. He ignores Jeliane.

"Good morning," Jeliane sings out. Russell doesn't alter his stoic expression.

"Some guy," Matt tells Russell. Jeliane waits for his order. Their silent standoff. She knows that he knows that she knows his order.

"What can I get for you today?" Jeliane asks.

She had time to put makeup on this morning so she's feeling particularly Kardashian. She wishes she could afford to shop at Nordstrom. Russell glares at her. She waits.

"A ten-ounce cappuccino and a double espresso," Russell spits out.

"Can I get a name for your order, sir?" Jeliane stares back at Russell, ratcheting up the standoff. Matt, who's already started the drink order, guffaws from the espresso machine. Russell doesn't answer Jeliane. Jeliane fills in *John Dope* on the iPad for Matt.

"What's her name?" Jeliane nods at the smoking redhead in his white Escalade.

"Never mind who she is."

Matt crafts a foamy whole milk, double-winged swan for the redhead. Yesterday he crafted her a rippled heart. The day before that, a stacked tulip on the surface of her ten-ounce cappuccino. *I'm rooting for you,* his latte art says. If it were Russell's drink, Matt would craft him a watery skim milk penis. *How do you like that dickhead?* his latte art says.

Russell pays cash for his drinks from a thick wad of bills, doesn't tip, and then steps over to Matt's counter to wait.

"What's on for today?" Matt asks amicably.

"I'm taking my snake out at the dog park."

"I hope that's not a euphemism, Russell."

Russell doesn't laugh. He pulls his cellphone out of his True Religion jeans and shows Matt a pic of him, shirtless and ripped with a huge snake wrapped around his neck like a tan and black diamond scarf.

"Can you take a snake to the dog park?" Jeliane asks.

"This is Tiny. I've had her since she was small enough to fit in my hand. She's an African rock python." Russell's face softens momentarily. The only time Matt and Jeliane will ever see that.

"Not Tiny," Matt comments on the ginormous size of the python.

"They are amazingly maternal," Russell says, showing Matt a photo of the massive python; her brown and black patterned body is coiled tightly around her eggs, protecting her progeny. Then he shows them a comprehensive album featuring Not Tiny's fierce love for her two-week-old snakelets. Neither she nor Matt ask what he does with the offspring. Both can envision an entire house filled with writhing, twisting pythons.

"She's my baby," Russell says. "Or maybe I'm her baby." He looks like he might weep.

"What, do you like to put her on a leash?" Jeliane is genuinely interested. "Is Not Tiny, like, in the back of your car right now?" Everyone peeks out the window to Russell's white Escalade. The redhead looks up at that exact moment and sees them all gazing curiously at her. She smiles and waves.

Matt places Russell's drink order on the quartz counter.

"John, John Dope," Matt calls out in his booming barista voice in solidarity with his bro Jeliane. Russell turns and scowls at Jeliane, not Matt.

Jeliane smirks at him. Russell takes his coffees and exits the shop. No goodbye, or thanks, or see you later. Outside the mall, Russell climbs into his SUV with the redhead, and sits idling.

"I'm going outside," Matt says.

Outside, Matt catches a glimpse of the cage in the backseat of Russell's Escalade. The redhead raises her cappuccino and smiles dazzlingly. Matt wonders if she notices the double-winged swan on her cappuccino. Russell glances sideways, then speeds off with the smoke show redhead in the front seat and Not Tiny in the back.

After Jeliane's eight-hour shift at the shop and four more hours at the university, the three kids above her basement suite run back and forth across the floor above her head. The single mother yells at them to stop, but they don't seem to hear.

"You should hear it down here," she wants to inform the mother. Jeliane vapes Lychee Lemonade out the open basement window. Her propane tank is in brazen sight like Sad Dad is trying to provoke her. He crosses the yard to the house and knocks on the upstairs door again.

"I need some smokes," Sad Dad says. Single mom is not impressed.

"I worked a double at the hospital today and it was my mother, not yours, not you, that looked after *our* kids. What did you do today?"

No answer from Sad Dad.

"Let me guess. You were tired because the garbage truck woke you up early, so you smoked pot, downed a bottle of Chardonnay, took an afternoon nap and roasted wieners for dinner?" Overworked single nurse mother is unsympathetic.

"No!" Sad Dad protests. "They were Bavarian cheddar smokies."

"What the fuck do you think I owe you, Bernard? You're lucky to have the trailer. No smokes." She slams the door shut hard.

Bernard! Sad Dad has a name. Jeliane hears the double click of the safety lock upstairs. Sad Dad Bernard stands a moment at the door, then sighs and plods down the stairs to Jeliane's door. He knocks politely. He knows she doesn't smoke cigarettes but has the occasional joint when Matt and her friends are over in the backyard.

"You don't look like a Bernard," Jeliane says.

"You heard that?" He grimaces. "Call me Bernie."

Too late, Sad Dad Bernard is already seared into her brain.

"What can I get for you today?" Jeliane switches SWF gear to barista.

"Have you got anything to smoke, miss?" Bernard asks. He clearly doesn't know her name and she isn't about to enlighten him. *Miss* will do.

"You won't like it. All Lychee Lemonade. No gas." Jeliane points her nicotine-free vape at him. Bernard puts both hands up in the air in surrender. He looks like he might consider a pull, but no way is Jeliane sharing her vape with him. She doubts he owns a toothbrush.

"A roach, anything?" he asks.

Jeliane checks the ashtray she leaves out for Matt. She picks up a couple random pot butts and gives them to Sad Dad Bernard.

"You don't have a snake out there, do you?" Jeliane motions towards the teardrop trailer with her vape. She shudders. Creepy Russell and Not Tiny come to her mind.

"No snakes. The odd mouse or two. Got a June bug the size of a cracker box right now, but no snakes." He rubs his arms like a sudden chill has come over him. *No snakes until the DTs set in*, Jeliane thinks. He grins at her. His front teeth are missing.

"I played minor professional hockey. My teeth are in the trailer," he says, reading the surprise on Jeliane's face.

She wants to shake her head at Sad Dad Bernard but nods instead. She remembers her propane tank.

"You can keep the propane tank." She wants him to know that she knows what he did. He looks perplexed. "The tank that I *just filled* that was *mine*."

He looks genuinely lost.

"For fuck's sake, you stole the propane tank from my BBQ."

"I'm sure I have no idea what you're talking about, miss." Bernard backs out the door, thoroughly affronted by her accusation. Jeliane draws deeply on her vape, so that Lychee Lemonade smoke wraps him in a dense cloud when she exhales. He looks positively crackers with his mashed-down hair and no front teeth.

Next week, she goes upstairs to pay rent.

"Can I look at your security footage from the backyard?" she asks the double shift-working mother.

"Sure," the mother says. So harassed and exhausted, she doesn't even ask why. She leaves Jeliane at the front door with her phone while she goes to herd her three children into the bathroom for their nighttime tub.

"Just put it on the kitchen table when you're done," she yells back at Jeliane.

Jeliane thumbs through the saved security videos. Sure enough, Sad Dad Bernard stumbles across the toy-strewn yard in the dark, unhooks her propane tank from the BBQ, and runs back across the yard with the tank pressed against his chest like a football. Halfway back to his trailer touchdown, he trips on the pink Barbie palace and hits the ground. Instead of getting up, he embraces the propane tank in his arms and blacks out. Subsequent videos show him lying motionless next to the Barbie palace. She scrolls further down the saved security footage. In the time-stamped early morning hour, he rises and lurches back to his trailer leaving the tank outside. Later, when he rises for the second time, he steps outside his trailer. His sleep-mashed face breaks into sheer, surprised joy.

Someone has gifted him a propane tank! He hooks the tank up to his Canadian Tire fire pit and gazes fondly at the house where he used to live. Where his wife and children live. Something like ex-wife love spreads across his unshaven face.

CALGARY, CANADA
1984

HAIR: THE CHRISTMAS MUSICAL

Elle drove to the casino that morning with her shoulder-length hair long gone. "Baby It's Cold Outside" by Dean Martin played on her car radio.

"Let's go short, baby. Like a tomboy," the hairdresser had suggested the day before. He gathered her long red hair in his hands and let it slide through his fingers as if to give her a second chance to change her mind.

"Short." She nodded her head.

"You've got the face for it, sweetheart." He cupped Elle's petite chin. "And your freckles are darling."

Elle laughed. He snapped his silver scissors in the air and sang along to Otis Redding's version of "Merry Christmas, Baby" on the posh shop radio.

When she walked into the casino that morning, Judy Garland's "Have Yourself a Merry Little Christmas" was on the sound system. She made her way to the pit stand. A merry little Christmas gasp from Wayne.

"Your hair makes you look like you're sixteen years old, Tiger," Wayne said, baring the white flawless teeth of his new dentures. The sight of Wayne's now perfect smile made Elle grin.

Elle smoothed her hand over her fresh hair, her Christmas present to herself. Last night her boyfriend, freshly stoned, pulled Elle onto his eager lap in the kitchen of their duplex and stroked her like she was a new pet. She hadn't expected that. It was just hair.

She went to the dealers' lounge. Erik and Amado rushed over. Amado turned her in a circle so he could see the new look.

"Do you love it?" he asked.

"I do," Elle said.

"Me, too," Amado said, squeezing Elle's shoulders. He offered her a Marlboro, which she accepted.

"You never do anything halfway, do you, Elle?" Erik said. Elle play-punched him.

Every dealer in the place had an opinion.

"Baby Cakes!" Moose wolf-whistled at her when she walked past to her table.

"Oh, Moose." She waved him off—only he could get away with that.

She stood at her blackjack table and watched The Crier and Billy Jacked, who were first under the tinsel-decorated metal gate. The Crier booked it toward his regular poison, the roulette pit. He pulled his toque off, and his field mouse-coloured hair went askew. Elle knew that after a certain point in the day, if the roulette was a bust, then he'd put his mouse head down and drip silent tears onto the red felt of the table. Hence his nickname. He cried most days.

Billy Jacked was severely underdressed for this brisk morning in December. The temperature outside was minus 17 Celsius with a windchill factor that made it feel like minus 25. Billy Jacked's hairless torso was visible beneath his open vest, which complemented his black cowboy hat and filthy blue jeans. No coat, no shirt, just his jacked biceps and pumped-up chest.

Today's casino cause was Adopt-A-Family, just in time for Christmas. The casino, like every mall in the city, was overrun.

Moose, former offensive lineman for the Calgary Stampeders and casino security tight end, halted Billy Jacked at the front entrance and pointed at the *No Shirt, No Shoes, No Service* sign.

"It's Christmas for Christ's sake, Billy. You need a goddamn shirt."

Billy Jacked maintained direct eye contact with Moose while he snapped his pearl buttons shut. A tantalizing reverse strip show. A sleeveless leather vest clipped up became a shirt.

"Just go in." Moose rolled his eyes. Whatever else Billy Jacked was, he was clever and had a sense of humour. He plunked himself down at Elle's table. He pulled damp dollar bills out one at a time from his crotch region, not his pockets. Elle used the plastic money-plunger to drag the genital-moistened bills across the green felt. She separated the bills without touching them. Unlike every other player who passed by Elle's table and commented on her short hair, Billy Jacked did not notice. She was relieved.

"Money change," Elle hollered at Wayne, who watched her from the pit stand. He understood why she wasn't using her bare hands to spread and count the crumpled bills. He'd tell the Adopt-A-Family volunteers to wear disposable gloves when they counted the box from Elle's table at the end of the shift. Everyone was so focused on Elle's hair and the amusing, repulsive shenanigans of Billy Jacked that day that they failed to notice The Crier in the roulette pit. "Last Christmas" by Wham played overhead.

"Thanks for nothing," Elle mouthed at Moose, who stood behind her table, possibly to make sure Billy didn't undo his leather vest and flash his chilled nipples at her.

Moose winked at her. He liked Elle. Whether with long hair or short hair, she was a good-looking redhead, sharp with cards and patient with even the most difficult players.

Elle fanned the four decks of cards, then coordinated her shuffle with Amado on the blackjack table across from her. Amado looked exhausted these days. Not getting enough sleep, he said. Erik, on the other hand, looked terrific in clean white shirts pressed by Amado, an amenity offered whenever Erik couched surfed. Even Wayne and George Apple were impressed. With Erik's black hair perfectly coiffured, he looked presentable despite his gnarled tie.

Elle spotted the trio of high rollers a few tables over. They never played at her table or at Erik or Amado's stations. She didn't know why. The Filipino mother and son never spoke to anyone outside Amado's quick nod.

Amado finished shuffling his cards and waited for Elle. Then they raced through the four decks, pushing the bad-tempered players to their maximum. After an hour, with no more sweaty bills to pull out of his crotch, Billy Jacked stood up on the rung of his burgundy pleather stool and hollered at the pit boss to come over like he worked there.

Wayne arrived and patted Elle's hand like the grandfather he was.

"Slow your roll, Doll-face," he said, but he knew what Elle knew. The more hands dealt, the more hands won. The anchor pulled out his wallet and gave Billy Jacked a couple of clean dollar bills. Billy Jacked smiled. Elle was relieved. No more crotch bills for the day. The anchor's generosity was a Christmas present to both her and Billy Jacked.

Wayne returned to the pit stand to resume his Styrofoam cup of burnt black coffee and his half-smoked Marlboro.

Elle continued to race with Amado, but less obviously. She glanced up and saw Regrettable Russell standing there. Well, damn. She'd hoped he'd be AWOL. His blue eyes gazed at her with detachment. She avoided looking at him.

"What the hell did you do to your hair?" he said, more than asked. A look of disgust on his face, like Elle had compromised some important male code. She didn't answer. He stood behind the table and continued to stare at her. He had on Liv's thick silver dog chain, which reminded Elle of her absence. She apparently worked at the mall now. It appeared she'd finally left Russell for good, much to everyone's relief.

After a certain uncomfortable point, Moose came back over from the front desk and stood with crossed, muscled arms beside Russell. Russell moved on. Elle mouthed another thanks at Moose, but this time she meant it.

Meanwhile, in the roulette pit, The Crier was in for twelve hundred dollars. He put his head in his hands and then left the premises.

An hour later, The Crier came back to the casino and slipped past the front desk where Moose was watching American college football. The Crier was unnoticed by the scrum of excited players. Elle didn't see him. Neither did Amado. Erik rarely saw anything beyond the clock after his last break. George Apple was buried in paperwork at his office desk.

But Regrettable Russell saw The Crier approach the roulette table. A sawed-off shotgun hidden at his side.

Russell bolted to the front desk.

"What's up?" Moose asked coolly, not a Russell fan and not happy at being interrupted from his football-in-progress. Russell pointed at the roulette robbery-in-progress. Neither Russell nor Moose could see over the dense scrum of blackjack players.

"Crier's got a shotgun," Russell said, matter-of-factly. Moose, for all the bulk he carried, moved around the desk with surprising speed.

The Crier approached the same roulette table where he'd lost his twelve hundred dollars. He raised the barrel of the sawed-off shotgun that he'd managed to slip past Moose. Moose would never get to watch daytime sports again. The roulette dealer and her chipper froze.

"I want my money back," the Crier said in a low, quivering voice.

"We don't have that. The cash cage has the money," the terrified dealer told him.

The Crier looked at her, confused for a moment, then lowered the shotgun and made his way over to the cash cage.

He raised his shotgun at the Adopt-A-Family charity volunteer, who, without a thought, pulled on her Rudolph the Red Nosed Reindeer sweater and exited the cash cage. Chuck Berry's rocking "Run Rudolph Run" followed her out the door.

In the quiet hush of the Games Manager office, George Apple looked at The Crier across his desk. Exasperation was written all over George's face, desperation on The Crier's.

"Why?" George asked.

"I wasn't going to rob your casino. I only wanted *my* twelve hundred back," The Crier said. George shook his head, his lips a grim line. They could hear the vibration of the players and dealers outside on the casino floor. Moose had sprinted across the floor and taken The Crier out, tackling and pinning him face down on the red paisley carpet.

The Crier rubbed his bruised, carpet-bombed face.

"He didn't have to be so rough," he said.

"He was a Stampeder linebacker," George said.

"It was for my family," The Crier said, gazing at his sawed-off shotgun, which was emptied now and propped up in the corner behind George Apple.

"For Christmas," The Crier said.

He put his head down on the desk and cried. George Apple rose and patted the man's back while they waited for the police to come and lock him up for his Adopt-a-Family Christmas. Adopt-A-Father. Adopt-a-Husband.

After the police escorted The Crier out the back exit, George Apple surveyed the casino floor. He caught sight of Elle's tomboy hair as she walked past him to the dealers' lounge.

"You used to be such a nice girl, Elle."

Elle flushed. She hadn't realized what an uproar her short red hair would cause.

"It's just hair," she said.

George Apple shook his bald head and smiled genuinely at Elle.

He caught Russell's seedy blue eyes across the casino floor. Liv's thick silver chain was a reminder of what Russell really was. Whether he liked Russell or not, he owed him one. For The Crier. For no casualties on his Christmas watch. Russell raised his arrogant chin at George with no expression on his face. Russell knew it, too. George Apple, casino owner, owed him one. George went back into his second home and shut his office door.

OLD MANILA, PHILIPPINES 1985

OPEN YOUR EYES

J-Mar left his studio apartment in old Manila in the down-on-its-knees part of Sampaloc. It was not to be confused with the lovely Spanish buildings further along the port: the exquisite two-storey hotel, the grandeur of the colonial post office, and the colonial hospital. Even the neoclassical Malacañang Palace had once been the luxury summer house of a fifteenth-century Spaniard who'd owned a fleet of trading ships.

Everywhere that J-Mar went, General Perez's men were sure to go. Like lambs, they followed him from work to night school to home.

J-Mar was in gridlock in his Corolla, inching along in traffic. He'd fixed his brake lights to avoid further interactions with Manila police officers. On this street, a skinny boy rode his red bicycle. A shirtless teenager hawked newspapers amidst the open-air Jeepneys. Young men in light trousers and t-shirts walked the sidewalk along with women in strapless sundresses beneath raised umbrellas.

The Jeeps lurched forward, taxis sped up along with the motorbikes and Mopeds, green Fords, orange Mitsubishis, blue Renaults, and a purple four-door Vauxhall. J-Mar's hell route to the Manila International Airport some thirteen kilometers away took him nearly two hours. Despite the disguise of his pale blue airport shirt and navy pants, he wasn't working today. He was his own decoy for Perez's men, who shadowed him in the black Jeep across the street.

Two men had stood close to him at Rizal Park last year when Ken Kashiwahara interviewed him. A cardboard sign was around J-Mar's neck then: FALL GUY. What did that interview sound like to the two men? It sounded like the NPA, the New People's Army, which J-Mar had joined shortly after Amado fled the country. It sounded like an armed communist insurgency stoking a revolution. Ken Kashiwahara nodded his head as J-Mar poured forth in a rush of words. He'd told Ken that the Marcos government had clouded the issue, deceived the masses. The Marcos version of Ninoy's assassination was not his, nor the fifteen other men dressed in pale blue shirts and navy trousers with bare feet. Rolando Galman had no more killed the Senator than a pig could speak.

"Have you ever witnessed a talking pig?" J-Mar asked the international journalist.

"No," Ken answered.

"Me neither," J-Mar said, "but I know a dead pig when I see one. So does Marcos. Dead don't speak."

"How do you know?" Ken asked.

Ken Kashiwahara did not believe the news stories and bogus court proceedings, which played out like daytime soap operas on the five Marcos-owned television stations. Still, without eyewitnesses to corroborate the truth, everything was fair game. The Crying Lady, disgraced, had fled back to Taipei.

"*I know*," J-Mar said.

Ken studied him, saw the intensity in the young man's eyes. His jet-black mohawk was brilliant in the afternoon sun.

"Open your eyes!" J-Mar said. "Look around you."

The pair of them surveyed the half a million people gathered in the park. They looked at the two men who were clearly out of place. The uncomfortable men shifted in their gaze. Ken Kashiwahara raised his 35mm and snapped a chance photograph that included the two suspect men. It would be J-Mar's future assurance that he would not disappear like so many others.

"Open your eyes," J-Mar whispered.

"I wish I could close them..." Ken Kashiwahara said, trailing off. The resolute baggage handler and the world-weary journalist shook hands much longer than was necessary.

J-Mar was still boxed in by buses and mopeds, the two men in their black Jeep in pursuit behind him. No one could stop, no one could move forward. Cars held no democratic sway here. Everything, everyone was equal. J-Mar glanced in his rear-view mirror. He saw the bad-mood faces of his tailgaters that were forced to follow the same topsy-turvy route. He lit a partial joint from the ashtray, took a couple quick pulls, then pulled off onto a side street to park. He left his tailgaters hung up in the path of the boy on the red bicycle.

J-Mar walked along the street to the Western Union. Inside, he picked up a money order made out in his name, Jejomar Rafael. The money order had no sender information, no return address.

Suddenly, J-Mar's pursuers made their presence known.

"Where are you getting the money?" the men asked.

"What money?" J-Mar said.

They pointed at the yellow and black Western Union sign.

"The money orders you pick up weekly."

"My uncle," J-Mar said.

"Who's your uncle?"

"Bob's my uncle," J-Mar said, grinning.

The two men didn't catch the joke. J-Mar watched an excessive number of American sitcoms, the only American programs Marcos allowed on his TV stations. No news from the outside world though.

"Where in Canada does your Uncle Bob live?" the men asked.

"French Canada," J-Mar replied.

"Where in French Canada?"

"Where they speak French," J-Mar said.

The men pressed further.

"Why is he sending you money?"

"For my honeys," J-Mar said, smoothing his hand over his slick mohawk.

"Expensive honeys," they observed from the generous amount on the money order.

J-Mar walked away, but not before they warned him that he may have to come in for questioning.

"By whom?" J-Mar dared them.

"Certain people."

"What people?"

They didn't answer.

"Your little sister goes to Estevan Adaba High, right?" one of the men asked.

"Yeah?" J-Mar said. The two men stared back at him.

"Pakyu," J-Mar said. *Fuck you.* "We know who you two fucks are as well. We know who your boss is."

"Who knows?" they asked.

He didn't need to tell them. They knew as well as J-Mar who the New People's Army were. A growing, armed threat to Marcos. The same communist organization that Rolando Galman had provided intelligence for on occasion. The same organization that had marched in Rizal Park alongside the nuns and the mothers, the teenagers and the priests, the doctors and lawyers, fish sellers and cab drivers. The power of ordinary people. Except the NPA was armed. J-Mar had numbers on his side. And thanks to Ken Kashiwahara, the American journalist, he also had a documented photograph of the two men. These two, from what J-Mar could see, had nothing. Otherwise, they would have picked him up a long time ago.

J-Mar strode into the slow-moving cram of cars and horns and packed Jeepneys. The two men didn't follow him as he jumped into his Corolla and headed instead towards the Manila Zoo. Not the Manila International Airport. No work today despite the deceit of his uniform. Maybe they'd misread his work schedule. He was going to meet the woman from Sto. Domingo church. The woman who'd stopped him at Rizal Park. He was going to meet the pig farmer's live talking wife.

NOT FRENCH, CANADA
1985

ANATOMY OF THE HUMAN HEART

Elle's social experiment had gone badly. Six months later the bathtub was still filthy. Her boyfriend was perpetually stoned. He lived like palace royalty, didn't cook or clean for himself or communicate anything beyond his own self-swirling universe. Elle's lesson was demoralizing. *Don't do social experiments on people, they'll fail you at every turn.* She shut the bathroom door, then packed up her clothes from the duplex and left everything else behind and moved back temporarily into her parents' basement. Outside the initial shock on her boyfriend's face, she doubted he'd notice her absence.

Two weeks later, she decided she wanted her skis back.

"Will you come with me to get my skis?" she asked her father early that morning.

"I can't today but this weekend possibly." Her father finished the rest of his coffee and went off to wait in the Canadian Tire parking lot until they opened at 9:00 a.m.

Elle climbed into her red Honda Civic and drove over to the duplex and waited outside until she was sure her boyfriend had left for work. She tried the door, but it was locked, and her old key didn't work. Her boyfriend had already changed the locks on the duplex.

She stood a moment and debated her options. She could come back this weekend with her father, but she didn't particularly want to see her boyfriend again.

She wandered around to the backyard. It was fully fenced; no neighbours could see in from either side. The basement window was small but not so small that she couldn't slither through. She tested the window. Her boyfriend hadn't fixed the broken latch yet. Elle took her runners off. Feet first, she arched her back like a limbo player and slid through the basement window into the dark of the basement. She paused to listen for movement upstairs in case she'd been wrong. In case her boyfriend might be home. Wouldn't that be a surprise? The thought made her nervy. Elle squinted into the dim room. Basically, the same as she'd left it two weeks prior. She spotted her skis and boots in the corner. Tiptoeing across the cold concrete floor, she retrieved them and pushed them out the small basement window. Then a random thought. Why not look around? See if anything else beyond the locks had changed. In sock feet, she mounted the stairs. She peered into the bathroom. The tub was not filthy. Someone must have cleaned it.

In the room next to the queen-size bed that she and her boyfriend had slept and rolled around in for years, Elle found her boyfriend's gold band on the table, and beneath that, a pair of size ten women's shoes that weren't hers. She slipped her feet into shoes the colour of cut avocados. Too large for Elle. The woman was tall and gangly, no doubt. Not small and flexible, like the limbo player criminal that Elle was. She didn't bother taking the gold band back that she'd bought for her ex-boyfriend.

Elle unlocked the duplex door and left it open. He wouldn't notice her missing skis in the basement, but he'd notice the wide-open door.

Her father stood waiting in the driveway, reading the surprised look on Elle's face when she emerged with her Elan skis and boots.

"I figured you'd come without me," her father said.

"I found a woman's shoes. Already." Elle put her face in her hands and cried.

Her father waited in silence, then put his hand on her back.

"Everyone comes from somewhere," he said.

"What does that mean?" She raised her head and looked at her father.

"It means people have flipsides." He nodded towards the duplex, her unfaithful boyfriend, the appearance of female shoes. "When you have all the pieces of the puzzle, then you get to see the full picture, and it's not always what you think." Her father held her evenly in his gaze.

He wrapped his fatherly arms around her, so she understood it wasn't a lecture, just a sad life lesson, one of hundreds that she knew was yet to come.

"Come back home, Elle." She looked at the duplex for a long time, then got into her car and didn't look back. Her father followed her.

She didn't tell Erik or Amado at the casino, despite the closed fist of her heart. She ached to tell someone, but she wanted to curl up in the dank wilds of her parents' cement basement and heal before she came clean about her breakup. Every time she came home from her silent days at the casino, her father had done something new in the basement. The night before, she had noticed the pink and purple flowered Mactac her father had stuck over the various holes in the particle board ceiling. She laughed in the dark of her teenage bedroom. Her father's desperate attempts to make her stay.

"It's nice having you home, Elle," her father said. "Your mother and I are happy you're here."

She smiled but felt like a failed social experiment. As much as she loved her parents, no grown adult wanted to end up back in a concrete basement.

Back at the casino, the Heart and Stroke charity group stood behind the freshly installed bulletproof cash cage while George Apple held his head in his hands in the games manager office. He picked up the phone and, despite his trepidation, called the Edmonton attorney general's office in charge of gaming.

"That you, Bill?" George asked when he got put through.

"Bill Hatch at your service," Bill said. "What can I do for you?"

"Something's up here. Can you swing down and check it out?" George asked.

"I'll be down later this week," Bill said.

Right before he hung up the phone, George asked him what had happened to The Crier.

"Your Crier has been banned from casinos everywhere for the entirety of his sorrowful life. No sawed shotguns for life either. But no jail time. He got off lucky."

George waited for more, but nothing came. Bill Hatch, a former RCMP officer, didn't do casual conversation. That's what George appreciated about him. All business, no word play.

"Good to know, Bill. See you later this week."

George tucked the pile of blackjack pit cards into the top drawer of his desk. Each loss was roughly the same amount. Give or take $3000. That was the only dependable piece of the confounding puzzle.

Outside on the floor, Russell and his card-counting crew circled the blackjack tables like enhanced sharks. They stood back and surveyed a half-empty table, waited until the count was up, then jumped in with maximum house bets. Or they took over an entire table and played the minimum until the count was right, then piled onto their bets. They didn't always win, had roughly a fifty/fifty chance, which was why George Apple allowed Russell and his crew to freely roam the casino. Russell was not rash. He, like George Apple, had a tightly controlled bankroll to protect. Restraint was a rare commodity in any gambler.

There came a rare moment when Elle's blackjack table was empty. Regrettable Russell left his crew, came over, and placed a minimum bet so Moose wouldn't bother him. Elle shuffled the cards, avoiding Russell's intense gaze.

He pulled out a Player's cigarette, offered one to Elle; he knew she couldn't smoke on the table.

"Take one for later," he said.

"I'm good," Elle said, and dealt the cards.

Russell played the four decks without altering his minimum bet. This was not a business call, but something else. Amado watched protectively from across the pit, mouthed *mapanganib* at Elle. Elle nodded her head at Amado. She knew *dangerous* when it sat at her blackjack table. She knew dangerous when she saw the silver dog chain around Russell's neck. With her recent break up, and her boyfriend's lightning pivot to a tall(er) woman with size ten shoes, the chambers of her wounded heart had nothing extra to fight Russell. She merely endured him.

Russell watched her reshuffle the cards.

"You look tired, Elle," he said, not unkindly.

Elle didn't answer. In different circumstances, with no past knowledge of Liv's black eye, she might have caved to Russell and his quick, quiet intelligence, his unwavering binocular eyes that saw everything. "Everything okay with you?" Russell asked.

This was Elle's chance to unburden her sad, bursting heart onto Russell, who seemingly had no heart. She almost answered him.

"I really wish you hadn't cut your hair," Russell said.

Then he shrugged, opened his wallet and pulled out a wad of cash for a serious buy in. He meant business now.

Elle prepared her floundering heart for the onslaught of Russell's gang who sat down beside him. Wayne got up from the pit stand and stood beside her.

In slow motion she dealt the cards to Russell and his crew. They bet the minimum; they were consistent in the precision of their playing—what they hit, what they didn't, which mirrored the house. When the count was up, they wagered seven squares with maximum bets that made both Elle and Wayne's heart fibrillate. Elle held her breath, pulled two face cards and went bust. Wayne grimaced, held his swollen fist to his heart while Elle dumped her tray. Wayne retreated to the pit stand, smoked a hasty Marlboro and then ordered more chips. He and the Heart and Stroke volunteer, a woman in red leotards the colour of fresh oxygenated blood, waited with chip trays until Elle finished up the hand and pulled the cards to shuffle.

"Get the bastards," Wayne hissed in her ear. "Do the Vegas shuffle."

"What's that?" Elle asked. No one had taught them that.

"*Seven, seven, seven, seven.*" Wayne mimed splitting the deck into fours, then mimed each seven like Elle wasn't sharp enough to count to seven.

Rude Rudy showed up and stood behind the table. Regrettable Russell, in a surprising move, invited Rudy to play with them. Rudy was ecstatic. Elle seven shuffled the deck four times, which took forever. Russell smirked at Wayne. Wayne smirked back. Game on.

At some point in the game, Russell and his crew and Rude Rudy bet big. Elle busted again, so George Apple wandered out of his office and noted the entourage of excited bystanders. The house was losing. Hallelujah. Hail to the God of Gamblers. An infrequent event that allowed even the most downtrodden player to dream, to hope, to pray for their better days ahead. It was what kept them all coming back. The promise to make back what they'd lost. George knew that Russell's card counting raised his odds marginally. It was the reason George wasn't concerned. What they won today, they would lose back tomorrow or the day after, or next week, next month. The only true winner in a casino was the player that never came back. Not likely to happen with Russell and his crew.

At the table, Rude Rudy cheered every time Elle broke. Billy Jacked showed up to watch in his greasy jeans, fringed vest, and beaded choker. He had a renewed supply of crotch-moistened chips along with his dollar bills. *Great.* With Russell's cool blue gaze, the growing stack of black twenty-five-dollar chips in front of him made Elle feel like she might rupture. No matter what she did, she couldn't turn the table around.

Wayne patted the table with his pink bloated hand after each Vegas shuffle, adding his personal voodoo that did nothing. Then in a last-ditch attempt, mid-hand, he knocked the plastic shoe off Elle's table. Like fifty-two pick up times four, two hundred and eight cards were splayed out on the red paisley carpet. No accident on Wayne's part, Elle knew. Regrettable Russell and Rude Rudy knew it, too. They ruptured.

"Fucking C," Rudy yelled. Wayne was red-faced and desperate.

Elle wished she could sink down onto the cigarette-scarred carpet along with the cards. Moose came over and stood behind Rudy.

"It's okay, Baby Cakes," Moose said.

Rudy's curses were reduced to Jesus Christs and my God almighties. George Apple stood on the other side of Elle's table while Wayne introduced four new decks of unopened cards. Russell glared at George. An inexcusable offense and they both knew it. George stared until Russell backed off. He knew boxing matches were won or lost in the initial stare down. It was the same for casino matches. Elle fanned each deck onto the green felt, then shuffled endlessly. After Wayne's accident it took twenty minutes to restart the game. And when it did, the table was turned. The new cards were erratic, the count not sure. Russell's enormous gains turned to a steady downgrade. His fifty/fifty odds turned back towards the house.

Rude Rudy, well ahead, cashed out. Russell and his crew did likewise. They exited the table. Wayne stood at the pit stand, smoking one Marlboro after another. Before he left, Russell leaned into the table.

"You should join us, Elle," he said. His four-hour days, his seemingly consistent wins. He made more money than Elle could ever earn as a dealer. She could finance going back to art college, if she got in. She'd done the portfolio prerequisite and was waiting for an answer back. She could move out of her teenage bedroom at her parents' house and get her own apartment.

Elle looked at Billy Jacked ready to dive in after Russell's crew left. Good God almighty, she was exhausted. She wanted out. Every morning when she drove down Deerfoot Trail to the casino, she hoped that some disgruntled player, Billy Jacked specifically, had burnt the place down overnight so that she wouldn't have to work there anymore. Maybe Russell and his crew were her way out? She seriously considered his offer. If not for Liv's black eye, she might have. But how to ignore direct evidence of Russell's mapanganib?

"I can't, Russell. I just can't," Elle said.

Russell considered her answer.

"Your loss," Russell said. He cocked two fingers at her like a pistol and released an imaginary shot.

After debriefing at the Holiday Inn Lounge with Erik and Amado, Elle retreated to her parents' basement. A note was tacked to her bedroom door. Her mother had left a wrapped plate of home fried chicken and mashed potatoes in the upstairs fridge. The generosity of that seemingly small gesture reduced Elle to tears. She'd cried more this month than in the last eight years. Someone had made dinner for her instead of the other way around. Nuking the chicken in the microwave, Elle sat alone at the kitchen table in the comfort of the slumbering house and ate her warm chicken. She was never more grateful for her parents.

Back at the casino, nine hours into his twelve-hour shift and with no hope of recouping the day's losses, Wayne retreated to the canteen for his much-delayed dinner break. The Singaporean chef in the casino canteen served the best Asian food this side of China. Wayne, starving after the gambler fracas with Russell's crew and Rude Rudy, sat down in the empty canteen and ordered the number three combination.

Wayne still had three hours to go until the casino closed at midnight and then another half hour as he closed out each table in his pit. He dreaded the end-of-night results, didn't relish handing the pit cards over to George Apple who would, no doubt, shake his head and look at Wayne like it was his fault.

"Number three," the chef hollered from the canteen. Wayne picked up his tray and quickly worked his way through the authentic fish ball soup, then steamed dumplings dipped in pickled plum sauce. He finished off with the tenderest Szechuan chili chicken he'd ever eaten. He leaned back on his plastic chair and pressed his fist to his chest, his fist the approximate size of his twelve-ounce stinging heart. Heartburn, Wayne suspected. But no, instead, sudden cardiac arrest. He collapsed forward onto the Melmac plates, his heart as constricted as his fist. The best Singaporean chef this side of China rushed over from the canteen, then booked it towards George Apple's office.

Wayne was unconscious, his arms splayed out like wings on either side of the small table, the side of his pale face smeared with Szechuan chili sauce. George placed his fingers on Wayne's neck and detected a faint pulse.

"Call an ambulance," George told the chef. He signaled for Moose. Moose stood guard while George administered CPR. Moose tenderly wiped the chili sauce from Wayne's inert face with a paper napkin, his animal eyes shiny and brimming. A two-person rescue attempt. A two-person pre-memorial. When the ambulance drivers arrived, George Apple leaned back on his muscular firefighter haunches, panting and exhausted from his twenty desperate minutes of CPR. The drivers loaded Wayne onto the stretcher and wheeled him out of the casino, unconscious but breathing. The nighttime casino watched Wayne in reverent silence. Once he disappeared out the door, the game went on. Cards were dealt, ivory balls were spun, hands won and lost, futures remained uncertain.

As the ambulance sped down Deerfoot Trail with its red and white lights on strobe, Wayne's 3.5 billion beats over the course of his eighty years stopped. No medical intervention would get him to the West Coast, the retirement yacht he yearned for. Hope utterly abandoned his tender, stilled heart.

MANILA, PHILIPPINES
1985

COMRADE-IN-ARMS

Lina Santos spotted him before he saw her. His jet black mohawk shone in the sun at the Manila Zoo. On this busy weekday, troops of mothers pushed babies in strollers, while toddlers ran alongside giggling and speaking gibberish. The curious animals in the zoo were as interested in the children as the children were in them. A few truant teenagers walked around as well. Lina waited for J-Mar next to the tiger cage. A full-grown male Bengal was partnered with a female. There was a child's plastic swimming pool in the enclosure.

J-Mar's mohawk surfed above the crowd towards her.

"Magandang hapon po," Lina said, bowing her head when he appeared in front of her. Her formal *good noon* to J-Mar.

J-Mar raised his eyebrows, waited for Lina to extend her hand. When she did, he shook it gently.

"Mabuti po naman?" he asked. *How are you?*

"I'm fine."

Clearly, she wasn't. She observed J-Mar's pale blue shirt and navy trousers. She hadn't expected him to be dressed like that today. A shockwave rose through her body. J-Mar was her dead man walking. She resurrected Rolando's ghost. The wretched image of him in that pale blue shirt pierced by multiple bullet holes on the front page of every newspaper in every country.

"What?" J-Mar asked, alarmed at the terror on her face.

"Your uniform," she said. "My husband was killed in that. I couldn't attend his funeral."

"The real fall guy." J-Mar could barely believe it. "You're his wife."

He'd seen photos of Lina Santos in the Manila newspaper, read headlines that the pig farmer's wife was missing and that investigators looking into Aquino's assassination wanted to question her. Here she was, right in front of J-Mar. Her newspaper photo didn't do her justice. She was much stronger than she looked. He wouldn't have recognized her from the photo. A good thing, likely. If he couldn't discern her from the newspaper photograph, then no one else would either. J-Mar wondered if she was on the General's radar. She wouldn't be here if she was. She'd be missing and most likely not alive.

She touched his forearm lightly. He felt a common voltage.

"Did you know Rolando?"

J-Mar shook his mohawk.

"We didn't. But we know he was the fall guy," he said, referring to his fifteen fellow Fall Guys at Rizal Park. "Your husband didn't do it."

"You work at the airport?" she asked.

"Not today, but yes," he assured her.

"Were you—?" she didn't finish her question. J-Mar shook his head vehemently. Best not to reveal himself yet. He didn't know what she knew. He didn't want to out Amado.

Lina's eyes filled. She needed anyone close to Rolando at the time of his death. She couldn't bear the thought that he was a lone pig farmer without any allies on the runway.

"I saw General Perez," Lina said, when she pulled herself together. "That morning. He picked Rolando up."

J-Mar stood straighter at the mention of the General. The newspapers hadn't mentioned that fact. Only the mystery of Rolando Galman's armed presence on the runway

He gazed at Lina, admired her courageous resolve for showing up—he wasn't sure she'd come. She was the real deal. Like Amado. Testimony from the two of them could potentially bury the Marcos regime.

"NPR," he offered up in lieu of Amado. "I'm with them."

"AWAR," Lina said.

Opposite ends of the spectrum with the same goal. Oust Marcos. J-Mar was communist and armed, whereas Lina's organization was largely peaceful. They were true comrade-in-arms, like her Blessed Virgin Mary she prayed to each anxious night. Lina ached for the uncertain future. The weekly demonstrations had grown since the shootings on Mendiola Street. Rage morphed into outright courage, and Lina watched it swell. Crowds now well over half a million strong had shown up at Rizal Park. There was a push for Ninoy's widow, Corazon Aquino, to run in the next election. A quote from Corazon was buried on the back page in the ladies section of the Manila newspaper.

"*If* there were snap elections," Corazon had told Lina's women's group regarding her running. "And *if* there were a million signatures endorsing me, I would consider."

"What's this in the papers?" Corazon's mother-in-law asked the next morning.

"Oh mommy, don't worry. It won't happen. Marcos says there will be no snap elections. And one million signatures? The people are too afraid. That won't happen," Corazon Aquino had said.

Yet, the whispered word on the hot humid streets, in the rice fields, on the pig farms, at the markets, within the hallowed churches, said otherwise. They're rising, rising—the people, the signatures.

Corazon was their only hope. The people had been submerged under martial law for so long that they'd forgotten who they were. No more. The people were rising. Lina rose with them.

"What do you want?" Lina asked J-Mar.

"We want the same as you," he said, meaning the New People's Army.

"No, you. What do you want?" she asked.

J-Mar looked at her with his dark eyes.

"I want my friend back," he said. She recognized the weighty loss on his boyish face.

"Where is your friend?" Lina asked. Death surrounded her and she couldn't bear to add more bodies to her nightly mountain. Rolando's sister and countless more that she didn't know.

For now, the pair of strangers, odd comrade-in-arms, stood wordless. Neither would give up. Neither would give in. Here was safety for Lina, justice for Rolando, assurance for J-Mar and Amado. She'd march with J-Mar at every rally that presidential candidate Corazon Aquino would speak at.

At the Manila Zoo, the Bengal tigers waited out the afternoon heat beneath the shade of the gmelina trees. The sun dropped, housewives and babies and toddlers departed for home, the truant teenagers vanished as if into thick air. In the cooler air, the male Bengal dragged the plastic pool over and ripped it to shreds with his massive claws and sharp incisors.

J-Mar raised his brow once more at Lina. Instead of shaking his hand, Lina leaned out and embraced J-Mar briefly in her arms. He let her. She squeezed J-Mar, then released him. He didn't smell like ylang-ylang or swine; he smelled like high octane airplane fuel and sorrow. A lethal combination.

CALGARY, CANADA 2017

THIS IS HOW IT HAPPENS

Night shift Jeliane is by herself at the shop. The evenings are generally chill. No one wants to be fully awake and vibrating on caffeine after 5:00 p.m. except for the Tinder dates where everyone wants to appear livelier than they are. The in-mall restaurants with liquor licences are filled with exhausted shoppers and exhausted shop workers alike. Jeliane sees the Nordstrom woman flash past in black patent leather flats, a lime green wool blazer, and wide leg pants. Stupendous. She makes her way to Double Zero where a single serve artisanal pizza costs two hours of Nordstrom work.

Jeliane pours herself a glass of cold brew and opens her SWF book to study. She gets out her yellow highlighter and marks the important stuff. *Reaction to the Second World War. The men that had to leave the workforce to join the defence forces had returned and women were fired from their position, replaced by the men.* Jeliane feels her blood rise. *Women were expected to quietly resume their lives as loyal and subjugated wives. Housewives were estimated to spend an average of 55 hours a week on domestic chores. However, after having been independent of male dominance during the war, women didn't want to resume these roles, and this brought about the Second Wave of feminism in the 60s and 70s.* Jeliane scrawls *Fuck that shit* alongside the paragraph after she highlights it. She doesn't care who gets the book after she's done the course. If they don't feel the same way, they should.

"This is how it happens." A man's panicky voice breaks Jeliane's concentration. She looks up to see a twenty-something guy in a black frayed hoodie in the shop. He unscrews the lid of the sugar dispenser and dumps the sugar into the shop waste bin. Then he picks up the Billy Bee honey and squeezes the plastic bear into the bin, adding gooey honey on top of the sugar. He manages to pour half the creamer into the waste bin before Jeliane erupts.

"What the fuck, dude?" she yells.

Jeliane comes around the side of the counter. She can take him if she must. The guy skates around her like he's Wayne Gretzky. He punches the slick black bags of designer coffee beans on the shelf. Jeliane hollers at the security guard, who is at the Bank of Montreal. He weighs less than Jeliane. She motions wildly for him. He takes his time getting across the marble courtyard. The crazed man looks straight at her and the security guard and laughs manically, then blades out of the shop. The security guard stares blankly at Jeliane.

"Did he take anything?"

Speechless, Jeliane shakes her head. She points at the trashed coffee counter and the waste bin, which is on its side. A sea of single origin coffee beans is splayed across their cork floor.

"What? This isn't enough?"

"Want me to call the police?" the security guard asks. It's clear he's not going to do anything.

"I can do that."

Jeliane shakes her head at the inept security guard. The man in the black hoodie exits through the glass doors of the mall.

"This is how it happens." The man's demented final war cry. The security guard purses his lips. The best he can do.

"Nothing taken, so no harm done, huh?" He doesn't wait for Jeliane to answer.

He resumes his non-committal post at the closed Bank of Montreal. The mall management doesn't bother to keep tabs on their security. He could catch *Captain America: Civil War* at the mall movie theatre for the rest of his shift and they wouldn't know the difference. He could sit out in his 1998 Toyota Echo in the mall parking lot and drink Milagro Silver cheap tequila if he wants, which he does. Jeliane sees him when she's outside on a break.

Shaken, Jeliane stands at the shop door. After she quits shaking, she goes into the back room and retrieves a broom. She sweeps the beans into a pile behind the counter. She'll pick them up in the morning when she opens the shop with Matt.

For the rest of her shift, every time someone wanders into the shop, she flinches at the till. She breathes through her nose, then exhales loudly like a yogic lion to quell the adrenaline coursing through her SWF body. *This is how it happens*, she thinks as she sits on the cork floor pulling on her vape. *Shrunken women, exhausted and worn thin from the unhinged patriarchy. Guys punching coffee bags, security guards who don't give a fuck. The SWF war is far from over. It's a goddamn war on civility*. She'd settle for reasonability.

"What the hell happened here?" Matt asks Jeliane when she walks into the coffee shop late the next morning. Matt stands over the single origin beans swept into a messy pile behind the quartz counter. The coffee counter is trashed. The shelves are empty.

"Some guy."

Jeliane is too tired to explain.

Matt looks at her, his cow brown eyes gooey like the waste bin.

"I'll tell you after." Jeliane ties the waste bag and drags it across the marble mall courtyard to the garbage disposal. The mall walkers nod at her. She's as much a fixture at the mall as they are.

"Do you care if I make drinks today?" she asks Matt when she gets back.

"No probs, Jel." Matt finishes cleaning up the shop, then posts himself at the till. On the side counter she opens her SWF book. She's determined to start her paper. She buries her head in her book and underlines every second line. Everything that happened in the 1960s and 70s of the second wave seems significant.

"Did you know the US didn't outlaw marital rape *until 1993*?" Jeliane looks incredulously at Matt.

"That's messed up," Matt says, and turns to address two teenage girls with Louis Vuitton handbags.

Christ, their handbags cost more than her tuition at university. She spots Russell at the bank machine examining his bank slips. His brow is in a knot. She glances at the shop clock. He's late this morning; it's almost noon. She looks out the window. The redhead in the white SUV is paying close attention to Russell at the bank machine. Jeliane puts her head down and waits for the teenage girls' drink orders.

"Two chai lattes, 190-degrees with vanilla sweet cold foam on top."

"Can we get some water too?" one of the girls asks.

After Jeliane makes the chai lattes, she walks over to the sink and fills two transparent cups with water.

"Is that, like, *tap* water?" the same girl asks.

Matt suppresses a horselaugh. Jeliane picks up the two plastic glasses from the counter and dumps them down the sink. The Louis Vuitton girls stare incredulously at her. When Jeliane refuses to acknowledge them further, they pick up their lattes and leave the shop in a teenaged huff.

"*Like* is that tap water?" Matt laughs out loud.

"Fuck off."

Jeliane goes back to her feminist paper. She's tired and not in the mood for Matt's levity that usually buoys her up. Russell comes into the shop.

"Ten-ounce capp and a double espresso," Matt calls out to Jeliane.

She fashions the foamy milk on the cappuccino into a striking cobra for the anxious redhead outside. Something is different about her this morning. No scrolling through her phone today. This morning, she appears nervous, edgy, not her usual sunny self.

The shop has a line now—Russell can't shoot the shit with affable Matt, so he comes over and stands by the counter, glancing at Jeliane's open book.

"Whatcha studying?" he asks. A rare question directed at her. She looks directly into the icy squall of his blue eyes.

"Second wave feminism."

"Women reading about fucking women. Just what we need. Betty Friedan and Simone de Beauvoir. Equality, equal pay." How the actual fuck does he know that? Jeliane is shocked. She sees the highlighted paragraph in her book. ***Friedan and de Beauvoir.*** Whatever Russell is or isn't, he's a quick study. Matt, who is swamped with customers at the till, glances over at Russell's unexpected eruption.

"Men and women *aren't* equal. Women *are* inferior. Men are stronger." Russell's raised voice is emphatic. *That* isn't underlined in her book. He puffs his upper body up like a striking cobra. He is stronger, but his ignorance makes him small and stupid. Russell moves onto the travesty of gender-neutral pronouns and trans women in a full, unhinged tirade that makes everyone in the shop cringe.

"What? Now we have *they*? What the fuck is that?" Russell glares back at the lineup of customers This is the most he's said in two years and Jeliane wishes to some feminist God that she hadn't answered his leading question. Jeliane slams his drinks down on the quartz countertop. Matt is calling out a steady stream of drink orders from the till that she can't hear because of the inequitable roar in her ears.

"Got anything *else* to do today, Russell?" she says, her face blood red. When he refuses to move away from the counter, she wants to throw the hot drinks at him. Frightened customers keep their distance. She glances out the shop door for the hundred-pound security guard. He's stationed at the Bank of Montreal, but despite the level of Russell's elevated rage, he is not fussed.

"We don't got time for this today, Russell." She motions to the lineup of stunned customers, though no one says anything.

"You poor brainwashed little girl." His blue eyes are colourless with fury now, devoid of civility.

"What did you say?" Jeliane challenges him.

"I said, YOU POOR BRAINWASHED LITTLE GIRL."

At that point, the security guard starts across the marble courtyard. Jeliane stares back at Russell. Matt is hostage at the till with the lineup.

"Can you just leave now Russell?" Jeliane says. She struggles to hide the panic attack rising in her chest.

Russell doesn't move. The security guard edges closer to Russell, but it's clear that he doesn't register on Russell's radar.

She's never seen Russell's flipside. Now that she has, she's spooked. She thinks he might punch her in the face despite the line of potential witnesses. Jelaine's survival instinct is fully engaged now, and something tells her to disengage. She forces herself to release his laser beam stare. Then and only then does Russell storm out of the mall. The security guard follows him and holds the glass door open like he's evicting him.

Everyone in the shop exhales in relief, Matt included. Jeliane's arms and legs vibrate for a full minute before she calms down. She understands at that moment that shock prevents people from reacting. If she wasn't in the eye of Russell's maelstrom, she might not have reacted either. Still, she side-eyes Matt at the till.

"Thanks a lot for the backup," she says, and takes the till over from him. She's faster on the till anyway and Matt is the drink wizard.

"I didn't know what to say." Matt slinks sheepishly over to the Victoria Arduino Black.

Jeliane looks out the window and sees the redhead briefly. The redhead has a look of terror on her face as Russell speeds off in his white Escalade.

After work, Jeliane calls her mother and tells her about the creepy snake guy that went off in the shop.

"Be careful," Elle warns her. "Guys like that will go home, obsess about it, then come back with a sawed-off shotgun. Tell your boss. Get him banned."

Jeliane doesn't disagree. Now that her adrenaline has dropped, she's scared.

"Do you want your dad and me to come over?" Elle asks.

"No, I just need to sleep, mum. I'll be okay. Talk to you tomorrow."

Jeliane hugs her knees beneath the plaid Costco blanket. She feels like she dodged a literal bullet today. Or maybe she hasn't. Maybe he'll come back for her, like her mother said. Matt's name pops up on her phone, but she declines his call six times. She needs to sleep, bolster herself for the rest of the week of university and papers and SWF and the coffee shop that she doesn't want to go back to. She pulls the blanket up around her bare shoulders.

Her last thought before she drifts into sleep: This is how it happens. How women fall prey to male violence. The futility of their circumstances. She finds no comfort in knowing that.

CALGARY, CANADA
1986

THE TIME IS NIGH

George Apple stood in the roulette pit and watched the ivory ball as it whizzed around the mahogany wheel. Since Wayne's death a few months back, he found it hard to spend any time in the blackjack pits. There were too many tender reminders of Wayne. The overflowing ashtrays on the pit stand, the emptied Styrofoam cups of coffee, the Szechuan chili chicken he avoided ordering in the canteen. He couldn't help but feel that if he'd gotten to Wayne even a minute earlier, that he might have been able to save him. Guilt bore down on him at every turn and distracted him briefly from his prime purpose. Protect the casino's bank roll at all costs. He owed it to every charity group that stepped into his casino, and he owed it to Wayne to remember.

He caught sight of gaming agent Bill Hatch's thin, wiry body as he entered the casino. Bill's visit had been postponed with Wayne's unexpected death.

When the AG's office sent one of their agents down from Edmonton, something was amiss. Eagle-eyed Russell noticed Bill's entrance from his current position behind the blackjack table where the familiar trio played. The young white guy, the Filipino mother and her sunglassed son took over the whole table, playing the house maximum to not relinquish control to any other stray players. Russell was interested in joining them, but they weren't interested in Russell. Russell was nonplussed by their exclusivity; his crew was at work on another table, and he had nothing but time on his side today. He'd hang around until he found a gateway into the successful selective trio.

George and Bill were in the office. Bill flipped through the selective pit cards from the last year and mulled the similar losses at different tables every second day when the charities changed hands.

"I don't get it," said George. "I can't figure out what the common denominator is."

"Dealer?" Bill asked.

"Different each time." George ran both his hands over his shaved head.

"Card counters?" Bill asked.

"Don't think so. Even Russell's crew isn't this consistent."

"Cards?"

"The cards are fresh every second day. New charity, brand new cellophane-wrapped cards. Don't see how you can get around that," George said.

Bill studied the pit cards looking for possible clues, other than the fact that there was the same base loss from a different blackjack table every other day. With thirty-plus blackjack tables, it wasn't easy to pinpoint the how or why.

"Charities?" Bill asked.

George shook his head. Bill Hatch knew as well as George that it'd have to be syndicate-level crime to involve the multitude of charities that ran through the Alberta casino and was therefore highly improbable.

"Dealer theft?" Bill tried again.

"Jesus, they'd have to be constantly palming chips to get that amount every day," George said. "My pit bosses would have noticed that by now."

"What about your pit bosses?" Bill asked. The acidic look on George's face made Bill back off from that question.

"Remember that plump blackjack dealer who wore band-aids on her fingers all the time?" Bill Hatch asked. "She used the adhesive from the band-aids to filch chips from her tray, then hid them beneath her belly when she went on break. Had a player buddy cash them in for her. She went to Palm Springs three times, compliments of the casino before we caught up with her."

Bill laughed. Humour was mandatory in his humourless job. He was constantly dealing with the scourge of the gambler underworld.

"If not the dealer, not the cards, not the charities, then the players? Anything unusual there?" Bill asked.

"How would I know that? I can't guess which table it's going to be from day to day. I have no way of knowing who plays where and when."

"Something is definitely up," Bill said. "Let's take a walk."

The pair rose and walked out onto the casino floor. All eyes were on them.

Elle and Erik raised their eyebrows at each other and wondered what was up with the attorney general's man. Bill glanced at Erik's wadded tie.

"Is that a joke?" he asked George. George shook his head and put his hand up. Amado put his head down and concentrated on the cards, something he rarely did. Amado was such a nimble dealer; he could have dealt blind. Regrettable Russell stood behind the trio's table and watched them play. Nothing was unusual about the Filipino mother and white guy who played standard. They were consistent in their hits and stays, their bets remained constant, they didn't seem to be counting cards. The sunglassed son on the anchor was somewhat erratic. He didn't play to any blackjack norms, and yet, the chips piled up between the trio.

Amado and Elle were on the same break. They dusted off, clapped their hands together as they left their respective tables. They sat beside each other in the dealers' lounge. Elle stuffed her freckled face with yogurt and oatmeal and berries that her mother had packed in a glass mason jar for her. "Want some?" she offered Amado, who was quiet and smoked two Marlboros in a row. No smoke rings today. He shook his head at Elle's yogurt. She guzzled the last of her black coffee down, then jumped up to hit the ladies' room.

"See you out there," she said to Amado. Amado didn't respond.

Russell checked on his crew, then resumed his position behind the trio. They actively ignored him. George Apple and Bill strolled around the perimeter of the blackjack pits. Every dealer at every table put their heads down and feigned concentration.

"Pull the cards tonight on any table that's in the red," Bill instructed George. "I'll come back at midnight, and we can go through them together. Don't tell your pit bosses or dealers. That way we can rule them out."

George nodded and shook Bill's bony hand.

"See you at the twitching hour," George said. Bill Hatch left the premises, and every dealer sighed a collective breath of relief.

Behind the trio was Russell. The play that revealed the clue. The sunglassed anchor flicked his pointer and middle finger for a hit. On twenty. The dealer had a face card.

"You've got twenty, sir," the dealer reiterated. The sunglassed guy continued to motion for the hit. Russell leaned in. No one on the table said a word. Apparently, whatever the anchor did was of no concern to them. Fucked for sure when you were betting the house maximums. Who hits twenty?

"Twenty, sir," the dealer tried one more time.

The guy didn't flinch.

"Hit it," he said.

The dealer turned the card over and hit the player's hand. An ace.

"Twenty-one, sir," she announced, the surprise in her voice. No one at the table reacted. The dealer proceeded to pull her cards and busted. Russell nearly fell over behind the table.

"What the *fuck* was that?" he asked the solemn table. "Seriously."

No one answered him. The dealer looked up at Russell, her face contorted with confusion. At that, the trio rose, quietly collected their stacks of twenty-five-dollar chips and headed to the cash cage. Russell wanted to run after them. He walked the perimeter of the casino past Elle's table, past Erik's, who never paid attention to anything outside his wristwatch at the strike of six o'clock, past Amado's, who watched Russell like an assassin homed in on his target. Russell failed to notice.

He stood excited at George Apple's open office door.

"What do you want, Russell?" George asked. His face was sapped from fourteen-hour shifts.

"You'll want this," Russell said, a superior smirk on his face despite his apparent need for George Apple's stamp of approval.

George sighed and motioned him in. Russell shut the office door and pulled up a chair opposite George.
Hours later, Elle and Erik were debriefing their day shift at the Holiday Inn Lounge. Amado was oddly quiet and tucked into the corner of their leather booth. Erik still had on his off-white shirt and mangled tie. The punk rock bartender had been replaced by

an older, more reliable barman who wore a cowboy hat and played country music. "Desperado Love" by Conway Twitty played on the lounge speakers now.

"What's up with the AG guy?" Erik wondered out loud.

Elle sucked on her Beautiful, a gorgeous mix of Grand Marnier and Courvoisier. She'd applied at art college for the fall term. Something to look forward to beyond her teenage basement bedroom.

After months of singledom and the death of Wayne, Elle realized that her wounded heart was a mere drop in the West Coast ocean that Wayne never made it to.

"Did you see Russell go into George's office?" Erik asked. For a dishevelled man who didn't notice much, he noticed that. Amado watched him with pale gold eyes and sipped on his blond pale ale.

"I did see that," Elle remarked. "Can't imagine George had much to say."

"Yeah, but what did Russell have to say to George?" Erik leaned over and shook Amado by the shoulders.

"You with us, buddy?" he asked him. Amado barely nodded.

Erik hollered at the cowboy man tending bar. "Bartender, bring us a round of Beautifuls," he said, before pulling last night's tip money out of his crisp white shirt pocket. Elle wondered how much time Erik spent at Amado's as opposed to his Chevy Impala or his apartment. She didn't know why he bothered with an apartment.

"For my beauties. The time is nigh." Erik grinned, showing off his band of white teeth and his black coiffured hair. He was such a striking man when he smiled.

Meanwhile, back at the casino, beyond the twitching hour, George Apple and Bill Hatch pulled the cards from one specific blackjack table.

MANILA, PHILIPPINES
1986

PITCHFORK FEVER

"Show us that you have the support of your country, and we will support you," President Reagan said in a private telephone conversation. Reagan and his wife were close friends with Ferdinand and Imelda—they'd spent time together at the palace. Reagan was eager to dispatch any ill will directed at Marcos.

There was no mention of the 3,257 known extrajudicial killings, 35,000 documented tortures, 77 "disappeared," and 70,000 incarcerations under Marcos's democracy that would come out well after the fact. Confident that he'd win, Marcos geared up his men, his money, his media and called for a snap election. He had the necessary components to maintain power.

Presidential candidate, martyred widow, mother of five and an ordinary housewife, Corazon "Cory" Aquino canvassed the archipelagos with little more than a van, a loudspeaker, and a gaggle of pink-clad nuns on her campaign trail. Among the Pink Sisters were Lina and the women of AWAR, dressed in yellow. Lina watched the yellow confetti stream down from the office towers as they passed by. Yellow streamers on poles, fences, shops. People with yellow wrapped on their fists and threaded on their wrists boldly walked the streets. No more ribbons around oak trees but something different now. The yellow of audacity. The yellow of Laban.

Outside the populous cities of Manila, Davao Quezon, Caloocan and Cebu, Corazon toured the rural and remote provinces. The farmers stood in the middle of their lush green rice fields and raised their hands to shield the yellow sun to see Cory Aquino. Then they raised their pitchforks and shovels and cheered. Cory Aquino spoke softly into the loudspeaker and thanked them for their courage.

"You must not be cowed into voting for a regime. You are free to vote for whomever you wish," Corazon told them.

Amidst the cheering pig farmers, Lina conjured Rolando, no longer in the blue pale shirt with sixteen bullet holes but in his everyday farmer shirt muddied with pig manure. He was standing in their long-forgotten rice field, the row of yellow ylang-ylang in the distance, with his pitchfork raised high in the sticky sky. He was shouting to her, only her. She knew that in her shattered heart. She stopped in a crowd of women and doubled over, breathing in and out so she wouldn't collapse entirely. When she caught herself, she stood erect, ran her eyes over the pig farmers once more. Rolando was not there. She spotted her neighbours. Her last connection to Rolando, she longed to embrace them in the field, but she couldn't.

CALGARY, CANADA
1986

BEGINNING OF THE END

George Apple pulled the cards from blackjack tables that yielded the same consistent red. Russell seemed desperate to redeem himself, but George's big fireman heart would not forget the blackened ring left by Russell's fist on Liv's violet eyes. Nothing would excuse Russell from laying hands on a woman. Women were to be respected, protected in times of danger; they were meant to be loved, and in dire times, sometimes left, but never ever harmed. In George's case, his exes left with the big screen TV and the house or whatever new car George happened to be driving when the leaving took place. Still, after three wives, George remained a man of hope. A big soft man who remained confident he'd find the right woman.

But now, thanks to Russell, George knew what the missing piece of the puzzle was. Follow the trio: the Filipino mother, her sunglassed son, the sallow-faced Caucasian who looked like he hadn't seen the light of day since birth. George suffered from the same malaise. Too much casino, not enough sunlight.

At 2:00 a.m., long after the dealers, charity volunteers, and the cash cage tellers had gone home, George and Bill and an entire team of attorney general's men splayed cards out on the roulette table. They examined the back of each card with magnifying glasses, ran their soft office hands over the backs of the cards to feel for invisible marks, nicks—anything that would give them a clue. Not a goddamn thing was revealed by touch or magnification or the ultraviolet flashlight they used to detect counterfeit money. They placed the cards back into the plastic shoe and gaped at the visible half circle of a card that peeked out from the opening. They compared these decks with decks from another table. Nothing. Just ordinary decks of cards from what they could tell.

George looked at Bill Hatch, his eyebrows pressed in frustration. The AG's men were exhausted and antsy. The morning would come sooner than they wanted.

"What do we know?" Bill asked George. His RCMP training. Take it back to the basics.

"We don't know a godforsaken thing, Bill. We've got the trio. That's it."

"We don't know how or who. How did they do it? Who else is involved?" Bill asked.

"You can't arrest the trio for winning," George said, "no matter how erratic they play."

One-by-one, Bill Hatch and the gaming agents invited the blackjack dealers into George Apple's office at 11:00 a.m. the following morning. George sat silently in the corner and observed his terrified dealers. His pulse rose with each interview.

"Do you know them?" Bill asked each dealer regarding the trio. The collective shake of the dealers' heads. No one knew them.

They didn't talk to anyone. The gaming agents leaned forward in their chairs to lock eyes with the dealers on that question—a nervy lie detector of sorts. Which way would the dealers' glance? Left, or right?

Elle and Erik and Amado watched from the breakroom. Amado blew furious smoke and Elle counted the rings. Then she remembered Amado's different Filipino versions of "good morning" when he'd greeted the trio daily.

"Do you know them?" she asked him in the dealers' lounge. Amado avoided her brown eyes. He had up to fifteen consecutive smoke rings. Not his record of sixteen but close.

"Filipino sisters and brothers from a homeland of fifty-six million people? What are the odds?" Amado snapped.

Defensive, Elle thought, but she deflected her gaze and looked at Erik. Erik looked hungover again. He wouldn't look at her either. Maybe she was severely off base? Her father's *Don't be duped* played through her mind, but she dismissed it.

"Amado Barcelona?" the dealer who'd just been in George Apple's office asked. "They want you next."

Amado glanced at Erik and passed over his freshly lit Marlboro, Elle grabbed Amado's forearm; the yellow threaded bracelet was tattered from the years spent barely strung around his wrist.

"It'll be okay," she told him. His beautiful face didn't reflect that.

MANILA, PHILIPPINES
1986

IRON BUTTERFLY

Everywhere that Lina Santos went, she saw Marcos. It was election day, and the presence of his soldiers standing menacingly outside the voting stations was undeniable. The young soldiers smoked Hope Luxuries and Philip Morris Internationals with their guns slung casually over their shoulders. They looked as fresh and harmless as the teenagers at the zoo.

Radio Veritas, the only media in the country that was not run by Marcos, announced that over three million people had shown up for the election. On the air, Cardinal Sin informed the people that the Marcos troops numbered around two hundred and fifty thousand.

The nervous voters outnumbered the soldiers by ten to one. A mathematical fact that gave the voters a shred of confidence. The soldiers were armed, yes, but they were no match for a willful mass that refused to back down this time.

Lina searched the hordes of people for J-Mar. She didn't see him, but several New People's Army members guarded the voting stations. The armed men formed a human barricade around the polling stations to protect the voters. Only then was Lina grateful for communists and AK-47s—another force that kept the Marcos's teenage soldiers from raining fire and bullets on the people.

"We know where you live, where your children go to school, what time they leave the house," a pimple-faced soldier told an apprehensive father in the voter line. The soldier looked like he was still in school. Lina shuddered. Was it not enough to threaten the parents themselves? Did they have to threaten their children? It was one thing to stand up for yourself, Lina knew, but another thing entirely to risk the lives of your children. The teenaged soldier made her childless womb ache. If she had a child, she didn't know if she could find the courage to stand up, let alone fight.

Further along at the polling station, Ken Kashiwahara caught the wafting scent of deep-fried sweet potato smothered in caramelized brown sugar. Kamote que. His favourite, his weakness. He swivelled his head towards the toothless man's cart and saw instead Marcos's soldiers handing out hundred-peso bills along with pre-marked Marcos ballots in broad daylight; in full view of the US poll observers sent by President Reagan to ensure a legitimate election. Ken could scarcely believe it. He raised his 35mm and caught the soldier red-handed in a photograph that he relayed back to his news station as soon as he got back to his hotel. Corruption needed no guns, apparently, only money. Chaos theory caught in black and white on his camera. Ken's thought: *a butterfly flapped its wings in the Amazonian jungle, and subsequently a storm ravaged half of Europe*. The hapless things that changed the world. As a journalist, Ken witnessed that over and over. A handshake between a Jesus-loving busboy and Robert Kennedy. A toothless man with a cart full of kamote que. An unarmed soldier with marked ballots. Who could predict the effects of that? Ken hoped that the butterfly effect would ravage Malacañang Palace instead.

Lina saw the massive, restless crowds, and the clear message the armed soldiers sent to the uneasy voters. The tension was supercharged. The slightest spark of a lit cigarette, a flung match, the hapless flap of a butterfly's wing, could ignite the entire nation. Lina felt sure of that. Everyone, including the soldiers, felt the weighty presence of the US fleet ship in Manila Bay. No one could guess which side of the election the US fleet would fall on. Lina stood at the polling station guarding the ballots boxes with her life. She had to remind herself to exhale every half minute.

"This election is rife with corruption, intimidation, and outright voter fraud. So brazen, so desperate, so out in the open, the voters themselves can scarcely believe it," Jim Laurie reported from a jammed polling station in Manila.

Seconds later, a soldier, who looked no more than sixteen years old, knocked the microphone out of Jim's hand and kicked his cameraman to the ground. Jim bent to help the cameraman and connected with the underside of the soldier's combat boot. He and the battered cameraman lay on the hot concrete as the armed soldier destroyed their camera equipment.

Jim Laurie was fearful, in utter disbelief. If this was out in the open, it wouldn't be long before Marcos's soldiers opened fire on the voters. Given Laurie's experience on the airport tarmac, he had no reason to believe otherwise. He felt warm blood seeping from his head wound. The appearance of civilians armed with AK-47s was welcomed by Jim. One civilian sported a shining black mohawk. The young soldier retreated. The mohawk man extended his hand to Jim and helped him up.

"You all right?" J-Mar asked the journalist and cameraman. Jim took off his plaid sock and pressed it to his forehead. The cameraman looked at the scattered, broken pieces of his equipment. Without his camera and microphone, he was impotent.

"I'm going in to help the US observers," he told Jim Laurie.

Jim Laurie reached over and removed the journalist clip from the cameraman's shirt pocket.

"Best not to advertise," Jim told him. Both looked miserable, hapless in the flap of the iron butterfly's wing.

CALGARY, CANADA
1986

I'M SO VERY, VERY DISAPPOINTED

Amado sat across from Bill Hatch and the firing line of the attorney general's men in George Apple's small office. George nodded at Amado when he came in. Amado exhaled quietly to quell the unease in the pit of his belly.

The agents recorded Amado's name and AG number.

"How long have you been employed?" Bill asked, which Amado didn't have to answer because George Apple did.

"Amado has been with us for three years now. Hardest working dealer in the bunch," George said.

Bill shot a look at George.

"Amado Barcelona. From Manila?" Bill asked.

Amado nodded. George shot a look at Bill. Yes, two of the trio were Filipino, but there would be no racial profiling on George's watch.

"Did you know them?" asked Bill.

"Know who?" Amado asked.

"The mother and her son, that white guy."

The AG's men leaned forward, hoping to catch the response in Amado Barcelona's pale gold eyes. He kept his gaze even.

"As well as I know Billy Jacked," Amado said, no outward trace of being defensive, despite the spasm in his gut.

"Who is Billy Jacked?" one of the AG's asked, a sharpness to his voice. George waved his hand that it wasn't worth explaining.

Amado felt the tide shift from casual interview to serious interrogation.

"A player who keeps his money and chips in his crotch," George Apple offered. Despite the absurdity of that, no one laughed.

The AG's men leaned back to their former positions. Oh, that guy. Harmless enough. Few things or people escaped the attorney general's office. Eventually they'd get their man or woman.

"Did you or anyone you know have access to the cards?" Bill asked.

That was the question that lit the fire on George Apple's face.

"Every dealer in the place has access to the cards. What the hell kind of question is that?" George said.

Amado remained mute. He thought on his early morning shifts vacuuming the tables, clearing the ashtrays, putting the cards into the numbered shoes, then placing the shoes onto their respective blackjack tables. Never Elle's or Erik's tables.

"Did you or anyone you know have *unlimited* access to the cards?" Bill asked again. Despite the dismayed look on George's face, Bill wanted to hear Amado Barcelona declare it.

Amado didn't answer. He thought later that if he had protested, offered up some kind of lie, an explanation, that perhaps George would have backed him up. But he didn't. His mouth was set in a straight line, a hint of defiance in his eyes. Amado's reckless pride for his homeland. He glanced up and saw the realization on his boss's face. *Only* Amado had unlimited access to the cards.

There was a slip of sadness in George's eyes. He could not help him anymore. Amado buried his face in his hands

"I'm so very, very disappointed," George said, more to himself than to anyone in the room. He went silent for the barrage of questions from the AG's men that followed.

"Who are the trio? Where are they now?" Bill asked.

"Did you mark the cards?" another agent chimed in.

"How did you mark the cards?" Bill probed. "We couldn't see anything."

Only the sunglassed anchor could read the expertly marked cards; Amado raised his head to look at Bill. He knew the AGs would have had nothing on him if they hadn't detected the marks on the cards.

"How much money? How long has this been going on?" Bill continued.

Amado knew that if he answered, his admission would be grounds for an indictment. Bill continued to fire questions at Amado, who remained mute. Finally, Bill and his agents stopped. George tilted his sad face at Amado.

"Why?" George asked. "Why did you steal from charities for God's sake?"

The one question Amado burned to answer. For freedom, for my country. George might understand that, but Amado couldn't answer. He couldn't bear the look of regret on George's face.

At 4:00 p.m. the door of George's office opened. In broad daylight, Amado Barcelona was escorted out the office flanked by a posse of attorney general's men dressed in sombre blue suits. Bill looked triumphant. George looked despondent. Elle glimpsed Amado's wet face amidst the group of serious men.

In Amado's tear-streaked face, Elle recognized the face of a man-boy who'd emigrated to Canada to escape the Marcos regime that was frequently on the front-page of the daily newspaper. He'd taken the same blackjack course as her. She watched the grim procession. She could have heard a pilfered chip dropping on the paisley carpeted floor. The casino stopped mid-blackjack hand, mid-spin of the roulette ball, halfway through the metal-spoked *click click click* of the money wheel. Every player and dealer in the place watched.

The Attorney General got their man. No one gasped or spoke. All eyes were with their comrade Amado. Elle wished she could save Amado; wished she'd known about the flipside of her friend. She'd been duped. Amado's only saving grace was that the Attorney General's Office had no evidence to arrest him. Instead, what followed was public humiliation and a call to the Minister of Immigration courtesy of Bill Hatch. Amado lifted his head and glanced back at Elle and Erik on their blackjack tables. His wet face was plastered with regret.

"*Slow your roll,*" Elle might have whispered into Amado's tender ear, but seeing the depth of commitment in his gold eyes, she'd have whispered instead, "*Go get 'em, Tiger.*"

For Wayne, for the Philippines, for her beautiful friend, Amado.

MANILA, PHILIPPINES
1986

SNAPSHOT OF A REVOLUTION

When the polls closed at 3:00 p.m., Lina and the posse of international observers guarded the locked ballot boxes until the New People's Army arrived to transport them to the municipal warehouse for counting. They'd heard accounts on Radio Veritas of Marcos's soldiers strong-arming the boxes and destroying them in the rural areas where support for Corazon Aquino was robust. No one was risking that, least of all Lina. Cory Aquino being elected was her only chance to redeem her dead husband.

Lina and the AWAR women formed a circle around the ballot boxes. The horrific *pop pop pop* outside the elementary gym was immediately recognizable. A group of young soldiers poured into the school.

"If you don't leave, we will shoot on sight," the pimply-faced soldier said.

Lina saw the conflicted misery on his teenage face. The rush of hormones, the impulsiveness of his age; she knew he wouldn't hesitate. Lina and the women rushed out of the gym and then sprinted full bore to a nearby church. Lina's heart thumped so hard that she felt it at the base of her skull. She spied the bright pink of the nuns hidden among the pews, the yellow of AWAR spread out behind the altar. Everyone held their breath. Outside the church window they saw soldiers knocking cameras onto the ground and kicking media personnel when they bent to retrieve their gear.

Then the New People's Army flooded the gymnasium. The young soldiers dispersed. The NPA tied the ballot boxes together with ropes, then formed human chains; they loaded the locked boxes onto a bus driven by a good-looking man with a jet black mohawk.

"Mother Mary Jesus." One of the nuns crossed herself at the sight of the driver, his black mohawk glowing like a halo in the bright sun. J-Mar would deliver the ballot boxes to the municipal warehouse where delegates from nineteen countries would count them along with the nuns and priests. Where President Reagan could watch from the comfort of his white house.

J-Mar stepped down from the bus, his comrades armed with AK-47s funded by the weekly money orders from Canada. If a butterfly flapped its wings in Calgary, would it set off a storm in the Philippines? J-Mar didn't know what to hope for. Hope itself, perhaps. Certainly not the storm of civil war that could further ravage their broken country. But if it came to that, J-Mar was prepared.

One-by-one, they retrieved the locked boxes in the blind faith that Cory Aquino might legitimately defeat Ferdinand Marcos.

J-Mar spotted the US fleet ship in Manila Bay as they drove past, then the heavily armed Malacañang Palace where Ferdinand Marcos paced the marble floors. Imelda was holed up in her rooms full of Chanel, Dior, Gucci, and the Filipino-made Marlet shoes stamped with her own name. Three rooms filled with three thousand shoes, which under normal circumstances brought her ceaseless joy. She'd wander past the rows and shelves, touching the toe of each shoe as she went by. Now, she sat on the polished hardwood floor and gazed miserably at her collection. She could match each shoe with every presidential event. Each offered their own distinctive experience over their past twenty years in office. She knew that was coming to an end.

She felt the explosiveness outside the palace walls. She didn't need to see the millions of voters that still lingered on the streets waiting with bated breath for the final count. She peered out the palace window. Far more people were on the streets than the mourners who'd come out for Senator Aquino's funeral march years ago. The sadness of the country had come full circle now, Imelda thought. Ninoy Aquino, the man she once dated in college, was her fatal error in judgement. She gazed at the gold-braided Gucci heels she'd worn when President Reagan and his wife Nancy had stayed at the palace. Not mere political allies, not simply business partners with the prospect of shared profits, but friends. True friends, she hoped.

She watched the same US fleet ship in the bay that J-Mar had seen. Whether the ship was friend or foe was yet to be determined. President Reagan was not answering her husband's fervent calls. Their choices were stripped down. Fight or flight. She didn't know the answer any more than her husband, who paced the marble floors of his palace like a caged Bengal at the Manila Zoo. She feared leaving behind her beloved shoes, her privileged life. But if push came to shove at Rizal Park, on the streets of Manila, and the rural pig farms of the Northern provinces, she'd push Ferdinand to fight. You couldn't corner a tiger and expect anything less, could you?

MANILA, PHILIPPINES 1986

BOXMAN

J-Mar and his crew of NPA members guarded the door of the flimsy warehouse where the ballot boxes were stored. Corazon Aquino was in the lead, confirmed by international observers and thirty thousand Filipino civilian volunteers. The foreign journalists who still had cameras and equipment broadcast the results to the world. Lina kept a public record on a billboard outside the warehouse. Lina posted the numbers from each region. J-Mar and his armed comrades stood outside the municipal warehouse at the ready. Ready for what, J-Mar could not guess. Only President Ferdinand could unleash that beast.

When he released his military tanks on the EDSA freeway, the people pushed forward and met the tanks where they stopped. They knelt in front of the tanks and prayed, then stood and pushed against them.

"Go away," a dying woman in a wheelchair said. She had nothing left to lose.

"Go away," the crowd echoed.

Their mass formed an impromptu cross on the EDSA.

The soldiers in the tanks were paralyzed by the sheer number of people—the Pink Sisters, the Catholic priests resplendent in their white satin cassocks, children giggling and smiling alongside their sombre-faced parents. The god-fearing soldiers locked themselves inside the tanks. The children climbed the tanks for a better viewpoint. They waved tiny yellow flags in the tense air and held no fear in their small beating hearts. Hope was their default.

Back at the counting station, Lina climbed down from the billboard.

"J-Mar?"

Without hesitation, J-Mar pulled her into a hug. She felt his rigid body on high alert. She held him until the coiled muscles in his body and hers released.

"Are you all right?" she asked.

"Are you?" he asked.

Neither of them answered. They watched the massive crowds in the streets. No one was going home. Abandoned taxis and cars and Jeepneys and felled trees blocked the streets. The crowds sang and chanted to ward off the fear of potential bombings, shelling, and tear gas.

"I was there," J-Mar said to Lina.

"Where?" Lina asked.

"The airport," J-Mar said. "Your husband wasn't alone on the tarmac. He had my friend, Amado Barcelona. Whatever happens here, I wanted you to know that."

At that J-Mar raised his AK-47.

"The same friend that funded this." He pointed to his fellow armed NPA. "We have the same friend."

Lina's eyes widened. She opened her mouth, but no sound

came out. Amado Barcelona, her husband's comrade-in-death. She felt a flush of relief that Rolando Galman hadn't died alone, hadn't died in vain. Lina collapsed into J-Mar. A Pink Sister stepped up to the billboard and resumed the public count. It was too soon to exhale—too soon for anything.

J-Mar held Lina until her heaving chest quieted.

MANILA, PHILIPPINES
1986

TIGER

Ferdinand Marcos and Imelda Marcos in her red gown and silver Dior heels stood on the palace balcony. "Ferdinand Marcos is the winner of the presidential election," Imelda declared through a loudspeaker.

Lina and J-Mar looked at each other in the throngs of people camped outside the palace. She shook her head. How was that possible? J-Mar surveyed the line of armed soldiers that prevented them from rushing the grounds. They joined the swell of three million voices chanting in unison: *No more, no more, no more*.

Imelda's celebratory speech from the palace was drowned out. She stood back with her husband in disbelief at the frenzied crowd.

The Filipino are worth dying for, they chanted now. Imelda knew then that Ninoy Aquino's people would accept nothing less. The Marcoses disappeared back into the safety of the palace. The soldiers readied themselves.

"I am your new president," Corazon Aquino announced over Radio Veritas from her home on Time Street. Ken Kashiwahara and Jim Laurie, with a plaid sock still wrapped around his head, broadcast her news back to American soil. They'd been front and centre at her husband's assassination. Now they stood in Corazon Aquino's neat living room as she declared her presidency.

"I have won," Corazon told the country. The country roared back in victory. J-Mar hugged his NPA buddies and Lina. The crowd didn't stop cheering until half an hour later when Ferdinand Marcos appeared on his state-controlled television stations and denied Corazon Aquino's claim. The country recoiled in horror; the world held its breath. In the crowd, J-Mar and the NPA pushed their way through the mass of people towards the closest television station.

In his fear, Marcos hadn't thought to guard the stations; instead, his army surrounded the palace. The NPA rushed the stations and shut his broadcast down.

"After twenty-one years, Channel Four is back," a triumphant anchorwoman announced. Glued to their televisions and listening to Radio Veritas, the country thundered.

The butterfly's wing broke the tiger's bitter back.

Then General Ramos of the armed forces released Ferdinand Marcos's list of opposition leaders to be assassinated to the foreign press. The entire country gasped. The world exhaled. President Reagan was in his oval office. He'd been duped, caught unawares by Marcos's flipside.

Now Marcos's top minister, Juan Ponce Enrile, defected and joined General Ramos. The pair of them, holed up at Camp Aguinaldo, held press conferences from within. The foreign press surrounded them. So, too, did Marcos's armed, hostile forces.

That night, Ferdinand Marcos phoned his friend Ronald Reagan. The people outside the palace refused to return to their homes. Ferdinand listened to the phone ring and ring and ring. President Reagan declined to answer the phone in his white house.

At midnight, General Ramos and Minister Enrile phoned the Cardinal.

"We will be dead in less than an hour," General Ramos told the Cardinal. "We need your help. We need the people's power to surround us."

On Radio Veritas, Cardinal Sin deployed his disciples.

"Right now, get out of your beds and go to the chapel and pray with outstretched arms. We are in battle," the Cardinal said on Radio Veritas. "I'm sorry to disturb you at this late hour, but this is when we most need you. Support our two good friends, Ramos and Enrile. Show your solidarity in this crucial time. I wish that bloodshed will be avoided."

Lina, exhausted from the weeks and days and sleepless nights, rose from her single bed anyway, stroked her orange cat, then made her way out onto the still-crowded streets towards Camp Aguinaldo.

Her neighbours in Bagong Silang also heard the Cardinal's desperate plea.

The pig farmer and his wife did not know General Ramos, nor had they ever met Minister Enrile. The pig farmer looked at his lovely wife from the confines of their straw house.

"I think we should go," he said.

His wife gazed back at him. The wound of Rolando was still present in her amber eyes. She missed Lina, who was presumed dead after all these years. She nodded in the dim light. The farmer and his wife put on their rubber shoes, then emerged from their house at midnight, armed only with a single flashlight to penetrate the darkness. Neither had considered that this was an armed conflict. What might take a Mercedes Benz an hour and four minutes to traverse would take their horse and cart ten times as long.

They made their way through the dead of night to Camp Aguinaldo and stood arm-in-arm with thousands of others who'd heard the Cardinal's impassioned call. The people surrounded the Camp, protecting the two men inside. Neither the pig farmer nor his wife caught sight of Lina, who stood in the centrifugal force of the People Power that guarded General Ramos and Minister Enrile from inside the camp.

With no one in charge and an uncertain presidency, Marcos's soldiers stood confused. They'd been trained to shoot armed persons but none of the people here were armed. The people surrounding Camp Aguinaldo swayed in the early morning hours and sang Bayan Ko. Nuns raised their rosaries in defence against the armed soldiers. How could the soldiers defend the homeland against that? As the night wore on, the conflicted soldiers laid down their pistols and AK-47s. They stripped the bandolier bullet belts from their bodies, and accepted food and flowers, prayers and hugs from the civilians. Children wore yellow paper headbands around their small foreheads with "People Power" scrawled in blue ink. The children passed ripe mangoes from a bucket to the soldiers. Both sides were grateful for forgiveness, for mercy, for the lack of bloodshed.

Marcos rang the White House again.

"What do you think? Should I step down?" President Marcos asked.

Ronald Reagan didn't answer the call, but his underling did. The sting of that was compounded by the deathly silence in Malacañang Palace. He didn't know where Imelda was.

"He thinks you should cut and cut cleanly. He thinks the time has come," the underling said. The prolonged silence on the other end of the telephone was so long that Reagan's underling wondered if they'd been disconnected.

"Mr. President?" the underling asked. "Are you there?"

"Yes," Marcos said, his voice tiny now. "I'm so very, very disappointed."

Within the hour, Marcos heard the staccato of mechanical wings in the palace courtyard. Helicopters dispatched from the US Fleet ship in Manila harbour were landing. "Cut clean and take nothing with you," the underling had said. It was a detail that would haunt the Marcoses for the rest of their lives when they sought refuge on the Hawaiian Islands. The question of their friendship could no longer be tested after this fact. Reagan would also cut cleanly.

When J-Mar and Lina and the entire world saw the private chambers of the Marcoses in the weeks following their exit, their wealth, riches, gold and rooms full of designer shoes were on full display. J-Mar saw the custom Mercedes inside the Malacañang Palace and nearly lost his mind. The decades of money the Marcoses had pilfered not only from the country, but from the world bank, was incalculable, not to mention the secured loans that they would not be required to pay back to the US. When Lina read *The Guinness Book of World Records* years later, it was reported that the Marcoses had stolen over three billion US dollars for their personal use.

Imelda Marcos broke down in the US helicopter and cried for her most prized possession: a single pair of Filipino-made shoes stamped with her name in gold on their size 8.5 soles. Ferdinand Marcos held her hand, but she didn't hold it back. *The Manila Times* headline the next day read: "Marcos Flees." Lina watched young housewives pick up the soldiers' discarded AK-47s on the streets and pose with them, giggling in terror and exhilaration. The power of the gun versus the People's Power. Look who won. The housewives' relieved, smiling faces were plastered on every newspaper around the world. Corazon Aquino was ushered into Malacañang Palace. Her first order of business was to reopen the trial for her husband's assassination. Her second order was to declare herself Minister of Defence and General of the Armed Forces. She would take no chances. Her housewife instinct: Keep your house in order. She was the mother of democracy.

CALGARY, CANADA
2017

THE CHEAP MALL

Jeliane drives to the economical mall on the east side of the city with her mother."

You can buy the exact same stuff that we sell at the mall, except it's like half price here," Jeliane tells Elle. "Economics by postal code." Jeliane shakes her head at the state of the capitalistic world that she's been studying at the university.

Runners are reasonably priced at the Shoe Warehouse. Jeliane needs a new pair of trainers. Elle is looking for a pair of boat runners, the slip-on kind you might wear on a weekend yacht.

"Have you ever been on a yacht?" Jeliane asks her mother.

"Not yet," Elle says. "But there's still *your* future."

She grins to show Jeliane she's kidding about the yacht.

The Shoe Warehouse is the size of a football stadium filled with aisles of shoes beneath blaring rows of white, fluorescent lights. It looks more like a shoe morgue for last year's models.

"I'm going to grab a coffee. Want one?"

"Sure, get me a red eye. I'll be in here." Jeliane tucks her white blonde hair beneath her black toque.

"Aren't you too hot?"

"It's not about being hot, mum. It's about *hot*."

Jeliane juts her hip out like a Banana Republic mannequin.

"Oh Jellybean," Elle laughs. "Let me know if you see any yacht shoes."

Elle makes her way through the busy mall to the Starbucks. She passes an exotic-looking redhead. The two women gaze at each other, a weird recognition of sorts. The redhead smiles at Elle with her perfect red lips and bright white teeth. They pass one another, and then the redhead disappears into the throng of shoppers. The woman's hair is long and red, whereas Elle's is pixie short and red. She's got a doppelganger out here in the world. *Huh.*

When Elle gets back to the Shoe Warehouse, Jeliane holds up a pair of white slip-ons for her mother. She has a pair of neon orange Nikes tucked under her arms for herself. Neon orange is not in style *this* year, hence the discount.

"How about these?"

Elle slips on the shoes. They fit perfectly. She passes Jeliane her red eye coffee.

"Give me those. I'll get them. You have no money."

"You won't get your yacht if you keep buying me shit," Jeliane tells her mother.

"You're going to buy me a yacht when you're done with school," Elle teases. "Although I'd settle for a swimming pool."

"I'll probably be back living in your basement before school is over," Jeliane sighs.

"Oh, your father and I would love that, Jellybean."

"I love you mom, but no. *Just no.*" Jeliane laughs. "No more basement suites for me."

The gauge for adulting success is when you no longer have to live in a basement suite, or a trailer, which neither Jeliane nor Sad Dad Bernard have achieved yet.

Elle pays for the orange Nikes. They sit outside on a cement bench on the east side of the city in the warm yellow sunlight. Jeliane offers her mother a pull on her Blue Raspberry vape. Elle declines. Both women have their heads down admiring their new runners when the redhead and the man in the white Escalade blitz past them.

CALGARY, CANADA 1986

BE PREPARED

A week after Amado had been escorted out of the casino, Elle sat across from Erik in the leather booth of the Holiday Inn Lounge. Elle could not get Amado's tear-streaked face out of her mind. Erik still had his black messed up tie on. Both were stunned. She did not speak. Erik filled Elle in about what he'd known about the trio, the marked cards, the required sunglasses of the anchor on the blackjack table. Amado would switch and cue up the cards for the trio each morning in his native tongue, which Elle thought were variations of *good morning* in Tagalog.

"He's gone," Erik said, his eyes shiny.

The cowboy bartender bought them a complimentary round of drinks. A Black Russian for Erik, a Beautiful for Elle, a Harvey Wallbanger for Amado. The cowboy set the drinks on the red terry-clothed table.

"Where's your friend?" the cowboy asked.

The wound of Amado's absence was too fresh. Elle didn't know what to say. Had they been duped by Amado? Would she regret his friendship?

"He'll be along shortly," Erik said.

The cowboy patted Erik's hand on the padded table and left to tend the line of patrons seated at the bar. She downed her Beautiful in two quick quaffs but failed to feel beautiful. Erik would never wear a pressed white shirt again. Not without Amado. The expression on Erik's face was grim. He knocked back his Black Russian, then offered Amado's Wallbanger to Elle.

"No," she said, "you need it more than I do."

The despondency in Erik's dark eyes, the depth of his commitment to Amado, told Elle something she didn't know before. She hadn't realized.

Elle signalled to the cowboy bartender to bring a repeat of the drinks, sans the Harvey Wallbanger. Amado wasn't coming back anytime soon.

Elle matched Erik drink for drink despite her small stature, her 4.5 litres of blood heavily diluted by Beautifuls. Erik walked her out of the dark lounge into the cold February air. They waited on the curb for Elle's taxi.

"Will you be okay?" he asked.

"Will you?" Elle asked back.

Erik gazed at her for what felt like decades—the length of time needed to fully grasp flipsides. Erik's, hers. Amado's. Their close brush with a real life revolutionary.

"I'll be okay," Erik said.

Elle reached up and hugged Erik, then realized that his black messed up tie was electrical tape, not polyester like hers. His disguise kept getting better and better. Elle laughed in the dark.

"Fuck, Erik," she slurred. "You are something. I don't know

what yet, but something."

Erik exhaled cold cigarette smoke out into the black air. Elle's taxi pulled up. Erik opened the door of the yellow cab and poured Elle in. He gave the driver her parents' address.

"I'm going back to the casino to get our tips," he told Elle.

"Thank you," Elle said, although in retrospect, she shouldn't have.

MANILA, PHILIPPINES 1987

NEEDLE IN A HAYSTACK

Lina was in her airless apartment in Manila. She lifted the alley cat from her sweat-laden thighs and went out onto the street. She pulled on her silver mirrored sunglasses so no one could see her eyes. What was she looking for? J-Mar, possibly, though why here, why today, she had no idea. She hadn't seen him since Corazon Aquino had declared her presidency. Since President Aquino had reopened the trial into her husband's assassination, and by extension, Rolando's posthumous conviction. They were two women united in daytime murder. Like an alarming soap opera, the story changed and morphed daily in the news.

She needed the true light of day back. She needed to take back the sixteen bullets that had pierced Rolando's pale blue shirt, breached his smooth, hairless skin that she could still feel beneath her calloused hands. *Then the horrible nothing.* That's what she needed. *Take back the wretched nothing.* Give Rolando back to her.

She needed to kneel at his gravesite. Tell him: *rest, my Rolando, lie down amidst our yellow ylang-ylang.* More than anything else, she felt indignation that the steely-eyed general was alive and well walking the same streets of Manila. She gazed down the thrumming street. Where the hell was J-Mar when she needed him most?

While the Marcoses lounged on a Hawaiian beach, their loyalists stalked the back streets of Manila, desperate to keep their skins intact. The unanswered question was who was the mastermind behind the assassination of Ninoy Aquino and murder of Rolando Galman? Amado Barcelona would testify to the presence of General Perez on the tarmac. He would identify the specific soldier who'd pulled the trigger on Ninoy. The pig farmer's wife could testify that General Perez had picked her husband up in the wee hours of a Sunday morning in exchange for a paltry bundle of pesos. The Crying Lady, with first-class rock-star seats, could corroborate everything. She was the missing piece of the trifecta.

Don't come, J-Mar told Amado in their last correspondence. *Lie low. Not yet.* It was the reason J-Mar had not seen Lina in the year after the People Power.

J-Mar needed to find the Crying Lady. Her face had been plastered on the front page of every newspaper around the world. Her sobbing was almost mythological. He'd heard from his NPA people that she was in Taipei. How difficult could it be to find one crying woman in a population of nineteen million? J-Mar's silver glinting needle in a Taipei haystack.

CALGARY, CANADA
1986

THE MORNING AFTER

The morning after the Holiday Inn Lounge binge with Erik, Elle stunk like unadulterated alcohol. The cheap kind that hollered inexperience. For Elle, youth and rawness were all that she had on her life front, other than a failed ex-boyfriend like a single notch on her bedroom wall. She opened the sealed letter her mother had left on her freshly pressed pillowcase. She'd seen it the night before but had been too piled with Beautifuls to read it. She'd laid her cheek on the sealed envelope and woke that morning with a sharp crease down her face like a pie chart. It was an acceptance from the art college she'd applied to!

She showered, changed into her casino black and whites, then kissed her momma's cheek. Her father went downstairs to fix the electrical outlet in her bedroom that kept tripping the breakers. Upgrades that her father hoped would keep Elle at home. She drove down Deerfoot to the casino, which wasn't burnt to the ground by an arsonist like Elle had wished for. Where others had imaginary friends, Elle harboured a straight-up arsonist. Her destiny rested entirely on Billy Jacked's instability.

At the casino, she sorted her cards and watched the stream of dealers roll in. The volunteer charity today was the Suicide Hotline. She reached up to her face to check that the straight edge of the envelope was gone from her face and felt a faint line that made her smile.

She spotted George Apple in his office. He'd rarely come out onto the floor since Amado's dismissal. He'd hired someone Elle didn't recognize to come in early and vacuum the tables. Not a dealer. Not Amado.

By the time she got out onto her blackjack table, Erik was still not there. George Apple paced the floor, his face a dark squall. It was not unusual for Erik to roll in at the last minute.

Erik was not here in hour one, not there in hour two, still not there by hour three. The dealers in the lounge buzzed with curiosity. Everyone waited on Erik for their tip money. All of them asked Elle like she had some special knowledge of Erik's whereabouts. Even George Apple cornered her on her break.

"I left him at the Holiday Lounge last night," she told George. Her defensive shoulders were up around her ears. Erik could be unreliable, yes, but to not show up to work without any warning was not standard fare for him. George Apple shook his bald head, walked back to his office, and left Elle defenseless as the day wore on.

When they realized that Erik wasn't going to show up to work today, the hum in the dealers' lounge reached a crescendo like angry bees in a hive.

"Maybe there's another reason," she told them. The dealers, thoroughly immersed in subversive gambler behaviour, rolled their pessimistic eyes at Elle. Regrettable Russell and his crew pulled up at the table next to her.

"Where's Erik?" Russell leaned over and asked Elle. Nothing escaped his card shark eyes.

"I have no idea."

The worst-case scenario buzzed in Elle's mind. She eyed the volunteers from the Suicide Hotline over by the cash cage. Could you call the Hotline for someone else? Could she stride across the paisley carpet and tell them: *I think my friend has done something serious. I'm worried about him.*

He's not at work today. He was despondent when I left him last night. *Why was he despondent?* they'd want to know. How to explain the tacit bond between her and Amado and Erik? Three disparate souls linked together because they'd all worked at the casino. How to impart armchair casino psychology to a stranger on the Suicide Hotline, or for that matter to the volunteer behind the bulletproof cash cage?

The Suicide Hotline would ask where Erik lived. The question Elle couldn't answer. *In the backseat of his Chevy Impala? The Holiday Inn Lounge parking lot?* Wouldn't that make Erik a perfect candidate for Elle's worst-case scenario? Both missed Amado. Not much to lose if you were sleeping it off nightly in the backseat of your car. She experienced a flood of gratitude for her parents' basement. What did Erik have but the prospect of another cold night in a parking lot?

She spent the rest of her casino shift avoiding the suspicious dealers. Everyone assaulted her on breaks, so instead of going to the breakroom, she went out back and smoked her Player's in the gravel parking lot.

Regrettable Russell followed her out, lighting his own cigarette.

"What's up, Elle?"

Russell stared at her. She did her best to ignore him, mindful of her fifteen-minute break. Moose poked his head out the door and nodded at Elle until she nodded back. Moose waited at the door. Russell crushed his Player's butt into the pea gravel and walked back around the building to the front entrance. He didn't want to be caught unawares by Moose in the unmonitored casino parking lot. He was not reckless. Moose held the door open for Elle.

"Thank you, Moose."

"Mind that guy."

Elle felt Amado's protective shield in Moose. She smiled back at him.

"Know where Erik is?" Moose asked.

Elle dropped her smile, fear on her face.

"I'm sure he'll be okay." Moose put his giant football hand gently on Elle's shoulder.

After work, Elle stopped by the Holiday Inn Lounge and checked for Erik's Chevy Impala, which was still parked in the same spot as the night before. Unslept in from the look of it. She ventured into the dark lounge and interrogated the cowboy bartender.

"Have you seen my friend?"

"Which friend?"

"The one with the black coiffed hair."

"Nope," the cowboy shook his Stenson. "Not seen him, nor your other man."

Dread filled her body. She understood the importance of Suicide Hotlines. She hoped to God that Erik did too.

VANCOUVER, CANADA
1986

WHAT WE DO IN THE DAYLIGHT

What was Amado Barcelona doing? The phone message from the Immigration Office sent him spiraling. Amado was lying low in a lightless basement suite in East Vancouver. His first day down Commercial Street, he saw a dude chasing another dude with a silver knife that glinted in the middle of the day. Amado checked his wrist for his yellow braided bracelet, which, after four years in English-speaking Canada, was gone. He missed the woven weight of it. He missed J-Mar. He missed his happy life in Manila.

The dude being chased had a sizable lead. The owner of Joe's Continental had the telephone pressed to his ear and was pointing excitedly out his window as the two men raced past.

Amado prayed to his God that the man being chased would maintain his lead. He kept his head down and headed to his day shift at the laundromat on Commercial where he gave out change, cleaned the dryer filters, monitored the popcorn machine, and inserted video cassettes into the VCR for the patrons. He also removed the unclaimed laundry from the machines and bagged them. After a month's time, if no one came to retrieve them, he brought them to a homeless shelter. He didn't understand that. Could you be so flush with clothes and money that you forgot them at the laundromat? For Amado, his wages barely covered his rent, let alone new clothes.

He couldn't risk going back to the casinos in Vancouver. The provincial casinos might communicate with each other. Or Immigration might follow up on their phone message. Bill Hatch had a bee in his AG bonnet that would sting Amado if he wasn't careful. Better that Amado kept his head down. He couldn't afford to do anything else.

CALGARY, CANADA
1986

MISSING IN ACTION

Elle was wrong. The cynical dealers were right. There was no other explanation. Erik was gone. AWOL. He had absconded with everyone's tips. George Apple and Moose made sure he was not dead. George called his landlord, and Moose drove over to check his dismal apartment. Erik's dresser drawers and closets were bare. No suitcases were found, and his unmade bed was dishevelled, much like the man himself. Moose noted the empty bottle of vodka and the sticky Kahlua rings on the coffee table in the dim living room. Suicides did not down Black Russians and pack suitcases.

Elle was at a crossroads. Art college. Casino life, single life. Over the summer months, her rage at Erik had subsided. It wasn't the tip money, but more the fact that he'd left her to fend for herself at the casino. She would see him again; she felt certain of that. For the next two years, she'd have to endure Regrettable Russell,

Rude Rudy and Billy Jacked on rotation like a bad Rolodex.

The day she moved out of her basement bedroom, her mother and father stood on the sidewalk.

"I'll only be in the Beltline," Elle said, soothing her sobbing mother. "It's twenty minutes away."

She caught a glimpse of her father's moist eyes beneath his aviator sunglasses.

The three of them stood on the street and leaned into one another for as long as they could.

CALGARY, CANADA
2017

WHERE ARE YOU, JEL?

Jeliane waits outside the cheap mall because she is meeting Matt for pho. She hopes Matt hurries up. He lives on the cheap side of the city while she lives on the cheap side of Varsity Acres—the difference is distinct. When she mentions Varsity Acres to anyone, they ask if she's a lawyer, an art gallery owner, a civil engineer, or a professor at the nearby university. No one asks you that if you live on the east side of the city. Jeliane has no idea why Matt commutes halfway across the city to the glass and marble wonder of the mall. The crap pay is the same whether he works there or not.

She raises her head to exhale a caramel cloud of Crème Brulée from her vape as Russell rolls up in his white Escalade. He parks in the handicap zone and goes inside to the Bank of Montreal. He's a man with a mission. Jeliane pulls her black toque down over her white-blonde hair. So, this is where he emigrated to. He hadn't shown at the mall since his superior white male rant. The redhead sits in the SUV with her window down, smoking two cigarettes back-to-back like she's nervous. Jeliane's never seen the redhead smoke before. She wonders if this is new. They both watch Russell at the bank machine. The bank slip comes out but there's no money. Russell tries twice more with the same result.

The redhead glances directly at her but doesn't smile or wave. She has no clue who Jeliane is in the context of this mall. Instead of going for coffee after the bank machine, Russell goes inside the Bank of Montreal and lines up for the teller. The look on his face is less than pleased.

A handi-van with an actual handicap tag pulls up behind the Escalade. The young driver leans on the horn. Heads swivel in the direction of the redhead in the SUV and the man inside the van in a wheelchair. Russell motions sharply with his hand for the redhead to move the Escalade like she works for him. The redhead slides over into the driver seat and pulls ahead to the fire lane.

Jeliane checks her phone for proof of life from Matt. He must be running late. *Twenty bucks he's still in bed*, she thinks. She finds a bench and suns her white-girl legs in the July heat.

"Fucking bitch," Russell yells as he storms out of the bank towards the Escalade.

Jeliane jerks her head. Is he talking to her? The cold-blooded savagery with which Russell moves compels her to remain quiet. She hasn't fully shaken Russell from the last time. Russell rips the driver door open and shoves the redhead aggressively over. The redhead tries to exit out the passenger door. When Jeliane hears the decisive click of the SUV locks, she bolts upright from the bench. She looks wildly around for mall security but knows instinctively they won't respond.

Russell pulls the redhead towards him in the SUV. He shoves the declined bank slips into her mouth.

"Where the fuck is it?"

Tears stream down the redhead's face. When Russell releases her, she spits the bank slips out and wipes her red lipstick off with the back of her shaky hand.

"You. Did. Not. Get. Fucking. Robbed," Russell says. He grabs her around the neck this time, while she kicks uselessly at the windshield. Female solidarity and bad judgement make Jeliane stagger towards the white Escalade. She doesn't know what to do, only that someone needs to intervene. Everyone else in the mall seems oblivious or drives past with no reaction to what's happening.

As Jeliane approaches the running vehicle, 6'4," 220-pound Russell straightens up and releases his sleeper hold. The redhead goes limp and slides down the white leather seat. Russell suddenly becomes aware of potential witnesses.

Russell looks like a King Cobra poised to strike. In horror, Jeliane glimpses the snake cage in the backseat. Not Tiny, the eight-foot python, and King Fucking Russell are in the same vehicle. Russell studies Jeliane's black toque, her blonde hair, her neon orange Nikes. His blue eyes narrow, holding Jeliane hypnotically in his gaze like he's no longer the cobra but the snake charmer himself.

Russell only needs to smile to make Jeliane's knees buckle. Jeliane breaks the hypnotic thread, raises her cellphone to dial 911 at the exact moment that Matt facetimes her.

"Matt," she screams into Matt's pillow-creased face on the screen.

She turns her phone as Russell speeds away from the mall. All Matt sees is a white blurred vehicle. He can't make out who's inside or why Jeliane is showing him this.

"Matt," she screams again. She staggers back to the cement bench while Matt tries to calm her over the phone.

"Wait for me," Matt tells her. She draws Crème Brulée into her lungs until the vape is empty. Terror forces her up and across the lot to her car. She gets inside and locks the doors. The extreme heat in the car makes her feel faint. She can't comprehend what she's just seen.

She drives shakily across the city to Varsity Acres. Sad Dad Bernard watches her rush past his teardrop trailer and through the toy-littered backyard. He recognizes the fear on her ashen face. It's how he feels each time he leaves his trailer to go knock on his ex's door. He lights a joint, takes a few quick puffs, and then pinches the burning ember off. He tucks a roll of scotch tape in his sweatpants pocket, then weaves across the yard to the basement door.

"You okay in there, miss?" he asks through her triple locked door. Miss doesn't answer. He wishes he'd taken the time to learn her name. *Something with a G or a J,* he thinks, but his perpetually stoned mind is blank.

"Miss? I've left you a gift." He scotch-tapes the half-smoked joint to her door. Bernard remains next to his daughter's pink Barbie castle and smokes his ex's cigarettes until the sun drops behind the Rocky Mountains. Then he retires to his teardrop trailer.

Jeliane watches him through her basement window. Despite the gnawing, knowing dread that roils in her belly, Jeliane feels Sad Dad Bernard's camaraderie and is indebted to him. After dark, she opens the door and finds the scotch-taped joint. She smokes it outside, but the pot and the bright stars in the black sky do nothing to quell her anxiety. She lies on the cool grass, then goes back inside and chokes down a stale bagel to ease her empty stomach. Nothing she does that night can obliterate the redhead's panicked face at the forefront of her mind.

The next day, Jeliane doesn't show up for her shift at the mall. Her phone buzzes incessantly. It's Matt for the first nineteen calls.

Over the next few days, she decides she will not go back to the shop at all. If she doesn't, then Russell won't find her, will he? She listens to the series of angry voicemails from her actual boss.

"*Where are you, Jel?*" Matt's voice is a desperate earworm in her head. She realizes she might be more than just Matt's bro. Her darling protective broflake. She'll lean hard on him in the coming months.

CALGARY, CANADA
1987

LINE IN THE PARKING LOT SAND

There are murmurs in the casino that management is no longer tolerating Russell and his crew now that they are winning more than they are giving back to Alberta charities. George Apple is fussed.

"He's hurting the bankroll," George told his silent partners. "The skinny bastard is too big for our britches."

"Get rid of him," one of the owners suggested.

"Not that simple," George said. "You can't just turf a player for winning. It makes the house look bad. The players aren't stupid, and neither is Russell."

George knew he would have to intervene, although he risked mutiny from the rest of the gamblers. A weird synchronicity among players that George didn't get. Their gambler code: the freedom to win, free-dumb to lose all your money. The latter worked for George.

"Keep an eye on him," the silent partners said.

"No fear there."

George watched Russell from the moment he entered the casino to the minute he cashed out. He knew exactly how much Russell won and from which table; how much time Russell spent at Elle's table when she was on shift. Due to his severe misjudgement of Amado's unseen flipside, Bill Hatch did some digging via money wires and found out that they'd had an actual revolutionary in their midst. Desperation begat desperation, but theft was theft, no matter the cause. George didn't think he had to worry about Elle flipping sides anytime soon. She was clearly creeped out by Russell. If Russell so much as parted his brown hair the wrong way, then George would kick his skinny ass out. Russell was a sharpshooter where cards were concerned, but he wasn't above tripping over his own feet.

Elle was on night shift now. Her art haven by day at the college was offset by her gambler hell at night. She put her head down and dealt cards. In a year and a half when she graduated, she could go around to every player in the casino who'd caused her grief and tell them to—well, she'd tell them something. She'd figure it out when she got there.

Her table tonight was full of pastel-haired ladies with their metal clasp purses. They'd pull out single dollar bills whenever they lost a hand. Never a full buy-in, just singles carefully extracted from their purses. A shuttle bus from the Evergreen Seniors Home on Macleod Trail had dropped them here.

"It's Seenagers Night in Vegas Alberta," the pink cotton-candy haired woman on anchor told her. "Seenagers, get it?"

Her too-white dentures sparkled at Elle.

"Adorbs," Elle laughed.

The women were a breath of fresh night air for Elle after the years of Billy Jacked and Rude Rudy and Regrettable Russell. She looked around the casino for Russell and his crew. Not one was in sight. They must have made their quota early and gone home. She noticed that Russell played later, stayed out longer now that Elle was on the night shift.

The pastel-haired Seenagers at Elle's table won and lost and won again, giggling their way through the evening. Her pit boss strode over to the table and whispered something.

"I need you at another table. They are getting slammed. You can turn it around." Her pit boss nodded in the direction of a table across the pit.

"No," Elle said to his shocked face. "I deserve this. Leave me with my ladies."

The ladies loved her, and they asked Elle questions about art college and if she had a special someone in her life.

"So daring," said the pink-haired anchor in relation to both Elle's short hair and her singledom.

"You'll live longer," the blue-haired woman in the middle said.

"She's ninety-six and never got married," the creampuff woman reported. They raised their Styrofoam cups of coffee in the woman's honour like she'd been the cleverest of them all. The spinster grinned. She had no teeth, nor did she bother with dentures. Elle could deal with this group for the rest of her casino career. She'd died and gone to gamblers heaven with these bright, wonderful women.

By the end of the night, the pastel ladies rose and were helped by the driver of the Evergreen Seniors' shuttle van. They waved raucously at Elle like they'd downed twelve tequila shots instead of Wayne's cholesterol-free black coffee all night long. Elle waved them out the door at midnight. Her table was the last to close.

Many of the dealers were already gone. The players never wasted any time vacating the premises once their window of opportunity was closed. The pit boss took his sweet-ass time getting to her table with the charity volunteer. She counted her chip tray, then all three of them signed the pit card; finally, she was free to go.

George Apple was at the cash cage helping the charity. Moose shuffled around the front desk, leaning on one leg, then the other. The minutes felt like infinity. George waved at Elle as she put her pink coat on and exited out the back door. She glanced around the empty parking lot in the dark, then made her way across the dim lot to her Toyota Celica.

Someone was standing beside her car. She tried to remember if prior to the Seenagers, she'd upset any players. Had someone lost badly at her table?

Her limbs tingled but she was ready. Whoever stood by her car, Elle could deal with them.

The person bent their head and lit a cigarette. In the flash of a Bic lighter, Elle saw it was not Erik or Amado. Not her ex. The familiar tall, stringy silhouette. Who else would stalk her? She flicked her cigarette into the black night and turned to face the yellow lights still on in the casino. Then she darted back across the lot.

By the time Moose escorted her out to her car, whoever had been there was gone.

"Think it was Russell, Baby Cakes?"

She hadn't mentioned that. Just that a guy stood by her car in the dark.

"I don't know. I couldn't see him properly." Elle was reluctant to confirm. She knew what Moose was capable of. She'd give Russell the benefit of doubt this time, even though he'd crossed the parking lot line.

MANILA, PHILIPPINES
1987

NATTY JESUS

Lina looked through the peephole. J-Mar's black mohawk was longer and higher than when she'd seen him a year ago. She slid the double bolts back on her door.

"I'm still scared," she said.

"I'm paranoid," J-Mar said.

Neither of them laughed. He stepped inside; an orange tattered cat rubbed up against his bare ankle.

"Friend?" He leaned down to pet the cat.

"Savior," Lina said. She reached out to embrace him. J-Mar flinched back. She understood his reluctance. They both missed their men.

"And I thought I lived in a dump."

J-Mar glanced around her three hundred square-foot apartment, which was a windowless bunker with a shared bathroom down the hall. At least J-Mar had a kitchen and a bathroom and a spare room in his hovel.

Lina knew it was a far cry from the hope luxury of her concrete farmhouse in Bagong Silang. The intense heat of her bunker forced her to go outside and mingle with the crowds on the street when she wasn't working in the refrigerated backroom of the butcher shop on the corner. She was grateful for the under-the-table, air-conditioned job. She knew pig like her native tongue. She could dress a pig down in less than an hour on her own.

"Where have you been?" she asked.

"Sampaloc in a Spanish castle." J-Mar joked.

Lina didn't laugh. They both knew the dirty roar of Old Manila.

"She's reopened the investigation," Lina said.

J-Mar had seen the headlines. The first-person account of journalist Ken Kashiwahara, brother-in-law of Senator Ninoy Aquino, was published in numerous newspapers. President Cory Aquino's investigation revealed that the shot couldn't have come from the pig farmer's .357 Magnum. The gun had not been fired, and the wrong calibre of bullet was lodged in her husband's brain. There were missing pieces to the puzzle. What had Ken Kashiwahara missed due to the blinding sun? What crucial pieces did the Crying Lady hold? Where was she? No one seemed to know or care now that she'd been discredited. Then there was the revolving door of credible witnesses that recanted their initial testimony and would no longer take the stand. Something had shifted over the past four years. Marcos's men had gotten to them. J-Mar knew that Lina Santos and the Crying Lady and Amado Barcelona could do serious damage in a courtroom.

"Do they know about your friend in Canada?" Lina asked.

J-Mar shook his head.

"I don't want to give Amado up yet. We need the Crying Lady. We need to find her."

"How are we going to do that?"

"I have the New People's Army. You have the women of AWAR. And I have the golden ticket. Free flights, perks of the job."

"I forgot about that," Lina said. She wasn't sure he still worked at the airport.

The orange cat leapt into her lap; she smoothed his fur down. Four years in her care and his coat was still natty. Four years and she was still afraid. Rolando's sister had been picked up shortly after the assassination and no one knew where she was. How could she hope for anything less than to also disappear? She looked across the small, lightless room at J-Mar. He studied her carefully, possibly gauging her mental health and the blackened circles beneath her eyes.

"Are you all right?" he asked.

"I can't sleep. I'm scared to go out except for work. I need to put this to rest." Lina broke eye contact with J-Mar. "This is all I have."

Hope was what she missed the most. She could grieve for Rolando and exist. But to lose hope was to stand with your toes on the edge of something fatal. No hope could be lethal.

"I can find the Crying Lady, then we can go to the courts together. My friend Amado will come back. I can put this to rest for you," J-Mar said, gently.

When Lina didn't answer, J-Mar got up and sat down beside her. He put his arms around her small shoulders and held her tight.

"It'll be okay."

"I just want to sleep again."

Tears leaked down Lina's cheeks onto the orange cat who licked them clean, like an apostle. She took her hand off the cat and cupped her tiny gold cross.

“Come,” he said. “Pack your stuff and come.”

“Where?” Lina raised her head.

“To my Spanish castle. You can sleep. I can do some digging. I have an extra room.” J-Mar pointed at the cat. “Does he have a name?”

“Natty Jesus.” Lina looked up and smiled for the first time since he’d been there.

“That’s brilliant, Lina.” J-Mar stood. “Let’s get you out of this cement bunker,” he said.

Lina lifted Natty Jesus up. J-Mar held him while she packed her clothes. She’d leave her meagre furniture for the next person—a kind of leg up that might give someone else hope.

CALGARY, CANADA 1987

BELTLINE

Elle's apartment in the Beltline on 17th Avenue came with a thin row of cotoneasters in front of her apartment, but she kept her blinds drawn. Tonight, on the cusp of a five-week art project that was due tomorrow, she worked late into the early morning on her airbrush piece. Her studio window was open to dispel the strong paint fumes. She felt light-headed and dizzy when she rose to finish her two failed airbrush projects. The pressures of art college were ridiculous. She wasn't studying to be a nephrologist. At best, she'd be a graphic designer or illustrator, if she was lucky.

She walked across the apartment floor to the open window to spray a final glaze over her projects. A crouched figure was outside her open window. Smoking and watching her. She squinted at the window, the stark light of her studio blinding her.

"Who are you?" she demanded.

A spark looped through her body like Tesla's coil. She couldn't see the man in the darkness outside her window. He extinguished his cigarette in the soil beneath his feet. Elle recognized the same cigarettes she smoked by their smell. Player's.

"I saw you from the bus stop," the man said, cocksure in his tone. "I wanted to see what you were doing."

Terror coursed up Elle's tense body. She needed to remain calm. He could easily slip in through the ground floor window or worse, reach in and grab her. She was so close to him that she felt the hair on *his* arms rise. If she escalated, then he might too.

The man rose from his haunches, then paused for a moment like he might be deciding something that Elle had no control over. Elle slammed the window shut and locked it. She stepped back and clicked the light switch off in her studio so that she caught the silhouette of the man as he disappeared into the black night. She didn't need to see his acne-scarred face. She held her breath until she finished shaking. She picked up the phone and called the guy upstairs who went to the same art college as she did. The young Swede had given her his number just in case.

"Can I come up?" she blurted when he answered the phone on the fifth ring. His voice was thick with sleep.

"Who is this?" The young Swede yawned.

"Me, Elle. I live below you. We go to art college together."

"Yes," he said, without hesitation.

VANCOUVER, CANADA 1986

I KNOW

The knock was unsure, perhaps testing to see if he was home and not at the laundromat on Commercial Street. Amado opened the door, thinking that his mild-mannered landlord had come to inform him that Immigration had called. No. Not the landlord. The man in front of him was immaculately dressed, had black slick hair and a sheepish grin on his face.

"Erik!" Amado pulled him inside the basement suite and shut the door. Erik looked around the sparse, immaculate room.

"Better than my Impala," he said, grinning. Amado smiled back at him.

"My friend." Amado reached up to touch Erik's perfectly styled hair.

Erik slapped his hand away. "Don't touch the Dutch." Then Erik held Amado's smooth chin in his fingers, turned his face this way and that in the dim light. He pulled Amado's body into his and felt the extent of Amado's fatigue in his slackened muscles.

"You feel like dogshit my friend."

Amado didn't disagree. The lack of exercise and the three hours of sleep he routinely got were to blame. He slept mostly at the laundromat next to a spinning dryer. It was how his mother used to get him to sleep as a child. The rhythmic *tickticktick* of the dryer soothed him then and still did. His mother was long dead, but he said good night to her each evening and missed her every day. When the landlord upstairs ran his dryer at night, Amado slept like his mother's child.

"I know," Amado said.

"Thank you for your letter."

Erik moved toward the single chair in the living room, a green Poang from Ikea that bounced when he sat down. "The Holiday Inn Lounge, though?"

"Your Impala didn't have a mailing address," Amado said. He hadn't stopped smiling since Erik waltzed through his sea-level door.

"I am happy to see you."

Erik ran his hand over Amado's chest, calming his beating heart. He glanced over at the coffee table, saw the blue and white striped envelopes with international postage stamped on them.

"Your NPA friend?"

Amado sank down to the floor in front of Erik. "Yes. J-Mar."

"What's happening?" Erik asked, even though he'd skimmed the world section of the newspapers daily for updates about the Philippines. He knew what Amado knew, but he needed to hear it firsthand.

"It's happening." Amado looked towards the one window in his suite. The light sharpened the dark semi-circles beneath his eyes.

"Will you go back?"

Amado wasn't sure. Nothing was secure in the Philippines. General Perez wandered the streets of Manila unimpeded by the police, or the courts, or President Corazon Aquino. The mapanganib General was still a force to be reckoned with. And despite J-Mar's efforts, he hadn't located the Crying Woman.

Erik got up to make tea for the two of them. Amado lay down on his Millennium Falcon carpet. Amado closed his eyes, momentarily eased by the presence of his friend.

When Erik came back into the living room with two cups of steaming green tea, Amado was passed out. Erik sat down in the Poang and sipped his hot tea. After he finished that, he drank Amado's too. He'd come with a purpose. He could wait.

He watched Amado, his hands balled in fists even as he slept. Amado could not rest or sleep or find love in this hellish in-between state. He had no choice but to go back. After an hour, Erik closed his eyes and slept. When he woke it was night. The two men had slept through the daylight. He lit a Marlborough, and the strong American smoke roused Amado.

Erik pulled a casino envelope out of the back pocket of his pressed trousers. Amado opened it and fanned the stack of money in the air.

"Where?" he asked.

Erik waved him off. Amado hugged him. Erik felt Amado's beating heart against his own.

"You don't actually have a choice," Erik said. "You really do look like shit."

"I know." Amado pulled back and laughed. Erik stood at the open basement door. Amado pulled him into one last kiss—a serious one.

"I love you," Amado said without thinking.

"I know," Erik said like he was Han Solo—Amado's personal Millennium Falcon to the rescue.

CALGARY, CANADA
2017

VARSITY ACRES

Jeliane hasn't left her basement suite for ten days. Not since she stood outside the cheap mall and witnessed Russell's rage with the limp redhead. She scrubs the bathtub and toilet with Mr. Clean until her head burns from the fumes. She scours the basement floor with Pine-Sol so her whole place smells like deep forest. She spends six days writing and rewriting her SWF paper and emails it to her university prof who reprimands her for being late.

She sends her boss at the coffee shop her resignation, which is also late. Her boss replies with three question marks and her termination papers. The papers are backdated from the second day she didn't show up for work. Never again will she bust her twenty-year-old butt for minimum wage.

When she goes to the cupboard, she sees that the bagels have gone green and that she's used the last of her single-origin coffee beans. She can do without the carbs, but she can't do without caffeine. She makes her way barefoot to the front of the house. She knows that if she knocks on the back door, the mother upstairs will think it's her ex and won't answer. Jeliane pulls Cool Cucumber from her vape. She's forgotten what real air smells like. The dawning sun soothes her exhausted face. She reckons she's had fewer than thirty hours of sleep over the past week. She hasn't spoken to anyone and has kept her phone off. She checks it now and sees forty-three missed calls from various people. She's too worn down to respond to any of them.

A young girl pulling a red Flyer wagon that Jeliane hasn't seen since she was five years old flings a newspaper towards the front step and almost hits her.

"Sorry!" the girl sings out as she whips past the sleeping house.

Jeliane waves at the girl, then picks up the newspaper off the front step and pulls off the elastic band.

Jesus fucking Christ. Russell's acne-scarred face and piercing blue eyes are on the front page of the *Calgary Herald* alongside a photo of the stunning redhead. Jeliane scans the article, but she already knows what horror it contains. She searches for the woman's name beneath her red-lipped smiling photo.

Verna Jones.

It occurs to Jeliane that she's seen this woman for two years straight and never known her name. She's from Malaysia. What a wretched way to find out her name.

Jeliane pulls her cellphone out and calls her mother.

"Jel?" Her mother's voice is drowsy.

"Remember that creepy snake guy I told you about at our coffee shop? The guy that came in every single day?"

Her mother, not fully awake at 6:37 a.m., can barely make sense of Jeliane.

"Slow down, Jellybean."

"The redhead that looked like you? The guy that went off on me at the coffee shop. The guy you said might come back with a gun?"

Jeliane waits for her mother to comprehend.

"Go get the newspaper, mom." She hears her mother pad across the living room, then open and shut the front door.

"This guy?" her mother says incredulously. "This is the guy? Holy hell, Jeliane Marie." Her mother only calls her by her full name when she's dead serious. "I used to work with him at the—"

Both mother and daughter read the details. The redhead is missing. She hasn't returned from meeting a "friend" ten days ago. That friend is Russell Braydon. The police have exhausted all footprints of life that a person has. Cellphone usage, bank withdrawals; then Verna Jones missed a medical appointment and didn't return home to her family. It didn't occur to Jeliane that the redhead might have a family. She wrongly thought that anyone rash enough to hang with Russell must have been desperate and alone, would have no living parents, certainly no children. This woman has both. Verna's last known location and photo was captured on CCTV footage from a mall on the east side of the city. Russell Braydon is charged with manslaughter and twenty-seven firearms-related charges. Christ, her mother was right. Russell could easily have come back to the coffee shop after his tirade with any number of his twenty-seven guns.

She reads further. Russell and Verna Jones are professional card counters. That explains Russell's daily trips to the Bank of Montreal. No wonder Russell is so cagey about what he does. The article says he's been banned from playing blackjack in Alberta. He plays poker in lieu of blackjack. That's why Verna Jones was with Russell. *Money*—is it ever about anything else? Money makes the world go around. Money makes the redhead *dead*. She can't read past that point in the article.

She has no words to tell her mother that she's witnessed the last breath of Verna Jones. Why doesn't she call the police now? She pictures Russell's murderous face at the coffee shop, in his

SUV. That's why she hasn't called the police. She doesn't have a death wish. Russell will find her. Of that she is terrifyingly sure.

"That motherfucker," Elle exhales over the phone. Jeliane has never heard her mother use that word before.

"When we worked at the casino, I used to share my cigarettes with Regrettable Russell. Like *give* Russell drags off my cigarettes. His lips to mine. He stalked me, too. If it weren't for Moose... Jesus, Jel, now I need a cigarette. I can't believe he's your snake guy. Christ, what are the odds of that?"

Who the shit was Moose? Why has her mother never told her about her casino days? What the actual fuck?

Jeliane studies Verna's smiling photo on the front page.

"She does look like me," her mother says like she's read Jeliane's mind.

The moment of their strange magnetic encounter at the cheap mall comes back to Elle in a lightning bolt.

"Oh, my god, Jellybean. *I saw that woman.*"

Jeliane doesn't know what her mother means. *It could have been you*, Jeliane thinks, envisioning her young mother working at the casino. *It could have been you*, her mother thinks, imagining her daughter at the coffee shop.

Jeliane's phone buzzes continually.

"Mom," Jeliane says "I gotta go. Matt won't quit calling."

"The police are looking for an eyewitness," her mother says before Jeliane hangs up and collapses down on the front step. Jeliane answers the persistent buzz on her phone.

"I can't even," Jeliane answers.

"Holy fuck, Jeliane." Matt says.

She can't talk to him right now. She hangs up and reads the rest of the article.

Jeliane scrutinises another photo of a woman taken from CCTV surveillance footage. An overhead shot, the woman has got a black wool toque pulled down over light blonde hair. Her neon orange Nike runners are highly visible. The newspaper warns that *Anyone who recognizes this woman is asked to contact the police.*

Jeliane slumps down on the front steps in the morning air while three child faces hold her in their anxious gazes. The children disappear, and a second later, the single mother appears at the door in silk baby doll pyjamas the colour of Icelandic glaciers. The mother pulls Jeliane's quaking body into hers. Jeliane buries her face into the nurse's ice-blue silk and sobs like a baby. She knows the police won't find the redhead. Russell is too smart and too slick—too piece-of-crap cunning. She clutches the newspaper in her right hand. In a matter of minutes, her phone is buzzing with her mother and Matt again. The nurse mother gently extracts her cellphone and shuts it off. The pair of them exhale in relief.

"Let's get you something to calm down."

The mother goes into the house and comes back with a half glass of Chardonnay and a tiny blue pill.

"Take them together," the mother instructs.

"You'll talk if you need to?" she asks when Jeliane rises unsteadily in her bare feet. The pill is working. The mother hands Jeliane her cellphone back.

"Leave it off," she commands.

Jeliane feels safe enough to retreat to her basement suite. In the backyard, she sees Sad Dad Bernard at the window of his teardrop trailer. She floats downstairs and triple locks her door.

She plunges into a drug-induced sleep. She dreams of women with shut eyes and of the indistinguishable faces of her mother and the redhead with no expression. And snakes, huge fucking snakes that fill entire rooms and guard their offspring with the ferocity of a female rock python.

CANMORE, ALBERTA
2017

BEAR NO WITNESS

Russell's picture is not yet on the front page of the *Calgary Herald.* For now, he drives his utility vehicle in the half-moon night. He's by himself but not really. His gaming partner is here too. He barely knows his own alias on account of the blur of sleepless days and nights since the mall on the east side of the city. His exhaustion is deep. He exits towards the Three Sisters lookout. The road looks remote, perfect for the pressing matter in the back of his white SUV. He peers into the red forest ravaged by mountain pine beetles. He doesn't see Grizzly Bear #122, but the Boss sees him.

Russell gets out of his vehicle and looks for camper vans, truckers, tents tucked within the dormant alpine forest. No one. The affluent town of Canmore sparkles below. He retrieves the Home Depot shovel from the SUV but doesn't look at his gaming partner. The thought of her gorgeous face and red flaming hair hurts his head. He has a job to do.

He digs a shallow rut. Enough to hold her. Russell leans on the shovel. Sweating, he smokes a Player's in the dark mountain silence. He crushes the butt with his heel and tucks it into his shirt pocket. He was never here.

CALGARY, CANADA
1987

WHERE THE CAMERAS DON'T SHINE

"Moose?" Elle said on her first weekend shift back at the casino. "Can I talk to you? "You bet. Anything for you."

Moose's eyes glowed like the monolithic animal he was named after. After she told him, he strode purposely across the floor to George Apple's office.

"Got a bone for you, Boss." Moose said at the open door. George looked up at Moose, rubbing his Game's Manager face.

"Somebody named Russell has been stalking one of our dealers."

He didn't mention Elle's name.

"Elle," George said. Russell spent most evenings glued to Elle's table. She certainly wasn't skipping her way to the casino anymore. George debated the pros and cons of Russell.

"Don't make me regret this," George Apple said to Moose. "We don't need any lawsuits." He meant the shipside of a favour he still owed Russell for averting the casino homicide last Christmas.

"Easy does it."

Favour returned, his debt to Russell paid.

"You got it, Boss."

Moose strode out of the office, nodded at Elle on the way back to the security desk. From his vantage point, he surveyed the players. No Russell yet.

Elle's pink lips were a grim line. She knew he'd show up. Russell couldn't help himself. At one point, she considered bleaching her red hair to a stark white, devoid of colour like the young Swede who lived above her. Anything that might deter Russell. She wished she had Moose's mass. The sheer physical presence of Moose when he'd tackled The Crier to the red paisley carpet was nothing short of terrifying. Every player in the casino witnessed that. Moose would not suffer dark silhouettes waiting beside his car at midnight, or someone crouched beside his apartment window at 4:00 a.m. in the morning.

After midnight, Moose waited beside Regrettable Russell's car in the parking lot. Billy Jacked was in the corner, sloshing gasoline from a red can onto the brick wall of the casino.

"What the hell are you up to now?" Moose yelled across the dark lot.

"Sorry, sorry, sorry," Billy Jacked said. Moose didn't know what he was talking about.

"Just feck off and go home," Moose said. "Don't do anything stupid."

Billy Jack crouched down and held his Bic lighter against the casino wall. A whoosh of yellow flame shot across it, then went black in the moonless night. The brick wouldn't take. Sensing Moose's animal presence five metres away, Billy Jacked stood up and grinned strangely.

Moose started towards him. He'd seen the flame. Billy took his leather vest off and frantically wiped at the gasoline on the wall.

"Jesus Murphy, Billy," Moose said, realizing now what was happening.

Billy Jacked threw his gasoline-soaked vest on and tossed the red can into the basket of his fixed-gear bike. Then fell sideways, sloshing more gasoline. Moose picked up his pace across the lot. Billy Jacked hightailed around the building.

Russell strode across the lot, the cherry red of his Player's cigarette burning in the dark. He jerked his head when he spotted Moose beside his car. Russell flicked his cigarette, which bounced off Moose's pickup truck. Reason enough for Moose to come at him. Moose loved his truck more than life itself.

Russell glanced around the empty lot. No cars, no witnesses, no cameras. Running would only prolong the inevitable. Russell didn't know if he could live with the dread of waiting for what was inevitable.

Russell puffed himself up with the idea that he might be better with his fists than Moose. He had no clue why Moose was out here. Too many nights fleecing Alberta charities with his card counting crew or too much animosity between him and George Apple. But why now, why tonight?

"Bring it, you big bastard," he muttered under his breath.

Moose sprinted across the lot and knocked him down with one insane hit. Stars swirled in the night sky, or in Russell's head. He couldn't tell.

"Stay away from Baby Cakes."

Russell stayed down, waiting for Moose's knockout blow. It didn't come. He didn't know that he had George Apple to thank for that. He'd never know.

"Who the fuck is Baby Cakes?"

"*Fucking* Elle. Stay away from her."

Moose stepped over him and headed for his pickup truck across the lot. The smell of gasoline lingered in the air. Russell cradled his loose jaw in his card-counter hands. What the hell did Elle have to do with this? Like every other woman in his life so far, she was a second-class commodity.

TAIPEI, TAIWAN 1987

CRY BABY

Lina and J-Mar landed in the city of Taipei. They only had to sift through some nineteen million people to locate the Crying Lady, but they knew that the Pink Sisters Convent had taken the Crying Lady in and hidden her from Marcos's loyalists during the first trial.

The small sister in her pink habit pulled Lina aside and confided in her. She eyeballed J-Mar, wary of his black mohawk.

"She's a professional mourner."

"What is that?" Lina asked.

"Actors paid to cry throughout the funeral. It is a sign of respect and loyalty to the deceased. If you want to locate your Crying Lady, go to funerals and visit the temples."

Lina almost laughed but seeing the nun's stern face, she refrained.

"Thank you," she said.

"Go with Jesus."

Lina gazed across the noisy Taipei airport. She wore a plain black dress and J-Mar had on a black crisp suit. With his mohawk combed down, he was transformed into a respectable businessman. Lina held a list of the city's Buddhist temples in her hand while J-Mar perused the rack of multiple state-run newspapers. He picked up the *Taipei Times* and flipped through for the obituaries. They had a grave and absurd task at hand. Find the Crying Lady, the professional mourner.

Days turned into weeks. Lina and J-Mar rinsed their black clothing in the sink of their cheap hotel room and hung them over the narrow balcony to dry. They'd visited so many ornamental gold and red temples, seen countless flowers and burning candles and brown-robed monks with their heads bowed in prayer. They'd attended the services of so many strangers that Lina could not keep track of them all.

Lina found herself welling up as if every funeral they attended was the service of her husband who'd not had that luxury. She had no idea where, or if, he was buried.

At one service, a woman dressed in white satin wore a white hood that concealed her face. She crawled on her hands and knees towards the coffin. Lina didn't know what she was seeing at first. J-Mar elbowed her sharply.

"A professional mourner!"

He recognized the costume.

"This deceased must be over eighty," J-Mar said. He pointed out the array of white and red clothing at this service. "A celebration, instead of grief."

Lina and J-Mar were conspicuous in their black wear. They tried to catch the hooded woman's face, but the veil concealed her identity. At the coffin, the woman threw herself on the ground and prayed.

Lina wondered how the mourner made herself cry. A seasoned actor? What private sorrow could conjure such convincing tears? The relatives pressed tissues to their faces now. Crying was a viral disease that everyone caught. J-Mar spotted the mourner's face beneath her white hood. She was younger than their Crying Lady. Even J-Mar teared up at her performance. Everyone here had lost someone, and the mourner brought them to their personal grief. Afterwards, the family bowed to the professional mourner in gratitude for her service. The absence of tears would bring disgrace to the family. Outside, Lina watched the young actor retreat to her car. A relative followed and passed her a bundle of money. She'd opened the floodgates for him. He was indebted. Lina wished she had a professional mourner for Rolando.

That evening, they walked the busy street in the Songshan District. Cars were banished from 5:00 p.m. to midnight for the grand opening of the Raohe Street Night Market. It was a much-needed reprieve from the weeks of funeral services. The wealthy area that once thrived had fallen into disarray under the years of martial law. The locals set up altars with candles, praying that the grand opening would reverse their misfortunes. Lina stopped to speak with anyone who would listen alongside the road.

"Have you seen this woman?"

She showed them the newspaper clipping of the Crying Lady. They shook their heads.

J-Mar bought a Yang crispy spare rib noodle while Lina treated herself to a mango rice bowl to sustain their search. They both indulged in the pepper pork buns, baked in deep round portable ovens and bagged hot. The sesame seeds on the buns sizzled and popped in their mouths.

Up ahead was the magnificence of the Songshan Ciyou Temple, which they hadn't visited. Lina pulled J-Mar away from the lineup at the glutinous rice hotdog stall towards the temple.

The towering roof was ornate with gilded figures of humans and flying dragons that existed on the same plane. A monk in a brown robe bowed his shaved head and greeted them at the entrance.

The temple was bursting with people who'd come to give offerings in exchange for karma and rebirth.

Despite her Catholic faith, Lina appreciated the bowed heads, the platters of food, the lit candles, the ocean of fragrant flowers. Spicy woodsmoke wafted towards the elaborate ceiling.

Lina dared to show the monk the newspaper clipping. He pointed at the altar up front.

"Go, go," he urged her.

Lina knelt at the altar and prayed for resolve, peace, and a chance to lay her husband to rest.

Outside the temple, people sat on the massive staircase of the temple talking, laughing, and sharing food from the street market. Lina went stair by stair and showed the newsprint picture. No one knew the Crying Lady. A couple thought she looked familiar, but they didn't know why.

J-Mar and Lina wandered back through the bustling stall and stood in line for a glutinous rice hotdog. Lina asked the people within the perimeter, then turned to the woman behind them dressed in white satin with a hooded veil pulled around her neck. Lina showed the mourner the picture.

"Do you know this woman? The Crying Lady?"

The woman took the clipping from Lina and examined the picture. She burst into explosive laughter. Bewildered, Lina and J-Mar didn't know how to respond to the woman.

"I know her," the woman said, catching her breath. "I am her."

Lina looked at J-Mar for confirmation. He leaned forward and examined the woman carefully. She stopped laughing and looked at J-Mar, serious now with her brown probing eyes.

"Yes. Yes. YES." J-Mar nodded, more definite with each yes. The woman suppressed a grin. She was hardly the melancholy Crying Lady they'd imagined.

The three of them stood beneath the sway of coloured lanterns. Without a word between them, they knew why the Raohe Street universe had brought them together.

CALGARY, CANADA
2017

BROFLAKE LOVE

Jeliane wakes in the dead of night in her Varsity Acres basement suite. Is it some disturbance from upstairs that wakes her?

She rises from her Ikea bed and pulls a pair of joggers over her turquoise thong. She arms herself with a succulent in a cement pot. She can beat the intruder to death. She peers out into her living room. Ghostly silhouettes of Skip the Dishes containers in the dimness are carefully arranged on her coffee table like a fast-food Stonehenge.

She glimpses shadowy movements outside the living room window.

Someone is there. The figure at the window leans in closer, pressing his face against her window. Jeliane lunges across the room and grabs her charging cellphone off the counter. She catches sight of the shock-wide eyes of the intruder as another indistinct figure moves swiftly across the yard and side-checks him against the wood house.

She turns the kitchen lights on. Sad Dad Bernard stands astride the figure on the ground. From the fierce expression on Sad Dad's face, Jeliane feels like he might squat down and teabag the intruder with his forty-year-old balls. Instead, Sad Dad Bernard trains his phone light on the intruder. Jeliane catches sight of Matt's sheepish face.

"Fuck, Matt, you scared the shit out of me," Jeliane yells through the thin window. Matt sits up and rubs his bruised face. He's got Jeliane's stolen propane tank wrapped in his arms.

"You know this fella, miss?" Sad Dad Bernard asks. He bends in closer and recognizes Matt. He leans down and gives him a hand up.

"Is that my propane tank?" he asks Matt.

"Don't. Even," Jeliane says. Sad Dad turns his head as if offended.

"Get in here," Jeliane orders Matt. Sad Dad Bernard looks excited like she means him.

"Not you," she says. Jeliane unlocks her triple-locked door and lets Matt inside. He hands Jeliane her propane tank and sways in the doorway. He's stupid drunk with a large red welt on his left cheek.

"Thank you for my propane tank," Jeliane says.

"I love you," he says solemnly, disarming Jeliane completely.

Matt sets his Tanqueray bottle on the kitchen table next to the messy stack of *Calgary Herald*s that Jeliane's been scouring daily. Russell's manslaughter charge has been upgraded to first-degree murder. Surely that means the police have something more concrete despite not having found Verna's body.

Matt sways beneath the bright kitchen light.

"It's you on the CCTV, isn't it, Jeliane?" Matt asks gravely.

"Things escalated."

Jeliane puts her head down like she might cry.

Matt hasn't gleaned what coming forward means—Jeliane putting herself within striking distance of a King Fucking Cobra and facing Russell in court.

"Oh, Matt."

She steps forward and folds herself into his eagle arms along with her propane tank.

"I'm so fucked."

CALGARY, CANADA
1988

THE GRADUATE

"No sign of him, Baby Cakes," Moose said. She didn't ask for the gory details; she didn't need that on her conscience.

"School done yet?" Moose came around his security desk and stood beside Elle. They both scanned the roving casino players for Russell's string bean torso. His crew was present but not their fearful leader.

"I graduate this year," Elle beamed. "I'm moving to Vancouver with my boyfriend in the summer."

"The twelve-year-old Swede?"

Elle punched him; his open hand caught her fist easily before it landed. He cupped her small fist in his large hands and laughed.

"You go, Mrs. Robinson."

That's what she loved most about Moose: his easy-going humour, his abrupt decisiveness when it came to business. She knew which side of Moose she wanted to be on. The Baby Cakes side.

Her graduation from Art College was so close, she could practically taste it.

On her last day at the casino, she'd go around to all the players that had caused her grief over the years and point her finger directly at them. *You're a dick. You're dispensable. You're history. You're banned.* The latter, the worst thing she could say to a player. She wished she had George Apple's authority to send those players packing. She'd include Rude Rudy in her dismissal, not because he'd caused her grief over the years, but because she wanted him to move on from the casino; wanted him to take his mother for lunch, find a proper girlfriend and shower her with a truckload of cashmere sweaters from his lucrative stockbroker salary.

"You're done, Rudy," she'd say affectionately.

VANCOUVER, CANADA
1988

WHAT HE WORE ON THE RUNWAY

Erik dropped Amado at the Vancouver Airport in his copper Oldsmobile. Amado turned in the passenger seat and gazed at Erik's dark, moist eyes.

"Don't," Amado cautioned him. Erik turned away, and so did Amado.

"It's all right," Erik said. "I'll see you again."

"If you say so."

Erik lit a Marlboro and offered one to Amado. An airport employee was hovering around Erik's vehicle parked in the fire lane.

Amado placed his hand on Erik's forearm. Erik tucked the cigarettes back in his pocket, then looked away.

Amado patted the envelope full of money in the pocket of his pale blue shirt. His passport was in the back pocket of his navy trousers. He leaned over and pressed his lips to Erik's. Erik didn't reciprocate. He didn't do public displays of affection, even in the progressive city of Vancouver. The airport employee grinned at the pair of them. Amado got out of the Oldsmobile and retrieved his backpack. J-Mar would meet him on the other end, and he'd be all right. J-Mar said he lived in a palace.

Amado leaned down into the open passenger window.

"Go get 'em, Tiger," Erik said, before speeding off, sparing them both the tearful goodbye.

Erik would never be far from Amado's mind. Erik was the reason he was at the Vancouver airport enroute to his homeland. Today was the first, best day of Amado's life.

He gazed out the Departures window and spotted Erik's copper Oldsmobile circling the airport. Maybe Erik had changed his mind. Maybe he didn't want him to go? Amado counted the ringed laps. Erik drove seventeen rings around the airport before he left. A new Guinness book world record—one more than Amado's smoke ring record. Amado smiled at Erik's warped sense of humour.

He heard the boarding call for his flight and slipped his backpack on. He would take Erik's victory laps back with him to the Philippines and hold onto them for as long as possible.

CALGARY, CANADA
2017

I GOT YOU, BABE

Matt scours the newspaper while Jeliane reads the Facebook comments on her phone. The Calgary Police Service post features the full CCTV video footage of the witness; Jeliane watches herself in her black wool toque and screaming orange Nikes. Thankfully, the cameras don't catch her face. Her overhead frozen image is juxtaposed next to Russell's sinister face and the missing Verna Jones.

They might finally have a witness!!!! Someone on Facebook comments.

Jeliane pours over the random comments.

Tragic. That poor woman. How did she get tangled with such a creep?

Do you guys remember this guy who shopped at Planet?? Sleazy dude with Ed Hardy or True Religion jeans all the time??

Omg yes... I remember now that you mentioned the Ed Hardy.

Soooo gross!! What a creep!!!

I know this guy; he was my very first enrollment at the gym I worked at ten years ago.

He was a card counter. He kept to himself, an unidentified casino person commented.

Known to law enforcement in Canada, CBC posted. *He also used an alias of Russell Elle.*

"Holy hell, he used my mother's name as an alias!" Jeliane tells Matt.

"Listen to this," Matt interjects. "Russell Braydon was granted bail last week. Among the conditions the Calgary man must live under while residing with his aunt in the 5600 block of Varsity Acres are 24-hour house arrest and the wearing of a GPS ankle monitor."

"Are you serious?"

Jeliane snatches the newspaper away from Matt. "That's less than seven blocks away."

A murderer out on bail? What the hell is that? She feels sick to her stomach. Matt's pale, hungover face blanches further.

"You aren't safe here," Matt says. "Come to my place?"

"Too small. No offense, but too hovel."

"What about your mom's?"

"With my tail between my legs?"

"Better that than missing or dead. Will you come forward?"

Jeliane puts her head down on the kitchen table.

"I don't know what to do."

She breathes into the cave of her folded arms. Her phone starts to buzz again. Her mother. No doubt she's seen the morning newspaper. She knows her mother and father will be frantic. Frankly, she's surprised that they aren't already at her doorstep.

"I can't tell you what to do, Jellybean. But if they don't find her body, Russell might go free ..." Her mother's voice trails off.

Jeliane cries into the phone and her mother's soft ear.

"Stay there, Jeliane. Your dad and I will come get you. Don't cry sweetheart. We've got you, babe."

Jeliane hangs up and Matt encloses her in his wingspan.

"I got you, too, babe," Matt says.

She can't find the right words to answer him.

MANILA, PHILIPPINES 1988

WHAT AMADO WORE ON THE RUNWAY

Amado's plane taxied toward the Manila airport, stopping at the Fated Gate Eight. Amado felt a red-hot sensation in his chest not unlike what he imagined sixteen bullets fired at close range might feel like. The Fall Guy. His Fall Guy. Amado's knees weakened, so he gripped the metal railing of the air stairs to keep from pitching forward. He did not regain his nerve until he spotted J-Mar's black mohawk coming toward him with two security officers in a pull cart.

"You will be ninety-seven years old and still have that mohawk," Amado said, skipping down the rest of the stairs and hugging his friend. "Jejomar. Jesus, look at you."

Amado pulled back and surveyed J-Mar. He'd put on a few pounds but was still his tight, compact self from loading luggage. There was just more of him.

"Five years of glutinous rice hotdogs," J-Mar said, patting his rotund belly. "You, my friend look like—"

Amado put his hand up and stopped J-Mar mid-sentence. "I

know how I look," Amado said. "It's good to be back."

Amado squinted to avoid the blinding sun; seven security officers maintained a circle around him on the tarmac.

"Are they here for me?"

"The National Bureau of Investigation sent them. Didn't think I was enough."

J-Mar scrutinized the other passengers coming down the air stairs. The passengers fanned themselves on the hot black tarmac while they waited for their luggage to be unloaded. They eyed Amado and J-Mar like they might be celebrities.

"Were you planning on working today?" J-Mar said, tugging at Amado's airport uniform.

The worried look on Amado's face made J-Mar go quiet. In his excitement, he'd momentarily forgotten the real reason Amado was back. In four days, Amado would appear in court and testify for the first time against sixteen soldiers, a murderous general and, potentially, an exiled dictator. The tall security officer nodded reassuringly at Amado.

J-Mar took the backpack from Amado and flung it into the cart. Amado noticed the same threaded yellow bracelet on J-Mar's thick wrist that he'd had.

"You still have yours?"

"New one." J-Mar spread his hands in welcome, motioning toward the cart.

"Harrison Ford doesn't even get this kind of treatment, my friend. Hop in."

Amado slid into the passenger seat. The two security officers hopped into the back. J-Mar floored it. A whopping seven kilometers per hour. It was slow enough for Amado to glimpse the bronze plaque in the exact spot where Ninoy Aquino had been assassinated. No such plaque for the pig farmer. It sent a chill through Amado's body despite the ninety percent humidity. He gripped J-Mar by the shoulder and squeezed him.

"Take me to your palace."

"Change of plans," one of the security men in the back said. "We've got a safe house for you.

"You're in for a treat," J-Mar said. "No doubt it's the luxury suite at the Pink Sisters."

J-Mar drove through the empty hangar to the limited access door. He used his airport pass to access the tunnel that led to the parking lot. His mango yellow, air-conditioned Mitsubishi was waiting outside. Two security men folded themselves into the tight back seat. Neither of them said a word.

The rest of security followed them in a white van with no windows except on the front and driver's side—the same kind of van that Ninoy Aquino had been whisked away in.

"They are good goons," J-Mar said, winking at Amado. "A few of them have been hanging around my Sampaloc palace."

J-Mar didn't seem fussed by the amount of security. As J-Mar drove up Roxas Boulevard, he turned the air-conditioner on full blast.

"Better than my Corolla that didn't have a bumper, huh? I'm moving up."

Amado laughed for the first time that day. He glanced back several times in the side mirror to make sure that they weren't being followed by anyone except for the white van. The security men were well-seasoned in surveillance. The tall man kept a close eye on either side while the white van brought up the rear guard.

After five years in wide-open, fresh-aired Canada, Amado had forgotten the flurry and close grind of Manila. The tropical air reeked of gasoline, and diesel-hot exhaust filled his nostrils like a familiar aftershave. He was back in his homeland. Amado surveyed the bustling streets and felt like crying. He'd been away too long. He was afraid to be back.

VANCOUVER, CANADA
1989

SEAGULL SPIT

Elle strode down the coastal streets of Vancouver where she now lived with the white-blond Swede who'd lived above her Beltline apartment. A familiar shape came down the street towards them. Elle recognized the dark, perfectly coiffed hair of the one man—the other she didn't know. As the couple drew closer, Elle saw him. Missing-in-action Erik found in the West End. As it turned out, if they both stood at their corresponding windows at the same hour of the day, they could wave to one another.

Elle steeled her mind to walk right past him, but as the couple drew closer, she couldn't avoid looking. She and her boyfriend stopped dead in their tracks on the narrow sidewalk.

"Erik?" Elle challenged.

Erik jerked his head up and saw her. His eyes widened in fear. How much reparation did Elle need? Here and now on the sidewalk of a coastal city, three years past stolen tips and the gut wound of missing friends, Elle examined Erik's turquoise belt that matched the turquoise pearl buttons on his shirt. She understood. Erik's way out was his way in. No dishevelled disguises were necessary in this city.

Erik's much-younger man surveyed Elle's boyfriend.

Elle reached up, tentatively at first, then completely wrapped her arms around her comrade's neck.

Erik stood stiffly until Elle released him. Then he opened his calfskin wallet and pulled out a small envelope with her name scrawled on the front.

"Of all people, I knew I couldn't avoid you, Elle," Erik said solemnly. "I saved this for you."

When Elle opened it, both younger boyfriends leaned forward on the sidewalk to see what was inside. She fanned the money out—her stolen tips.

"Erik, you are something else."

She side-eyed his good-looking boyfriend who was side-eying her good-looking boyfriend.

"Lunch is on me."

They walked to English Bay where ocean tankers the size of football stadiums floated in the distance. At the beach, only the sea-starved tourists swam in the ocean water. The locals knew better than to share water with oil tankers.

Erik ordered a round of Black Russians for their young men.

"And a Beautiful for my beautiful friend."

He felt a mountain of relief from their inevitable encounter. He'd dreaded it nightly. Elle was in front of him now and she was smiling. He could exhale.

"I'm working the casinos here," he said. "Six days a week on the money wheel."

The sardonic grin on Erik's face made Elle howl.

"It's fine, Elle. No one even pays attention to me."

Erik smoothed his black hair.

"I do," his boyfriend said.

"Amado?" Elle asked.

"Amado Barcelona. Our real life revolutionary. He was a baggage handler in the Philippines. Front row seats to a senator's assassination and the murder of a pig farmer."

Elle knew pieces of the story but listened while Erik filled in the details. It sounded like an international spy novel. She had no idea of the depth of Amado's commitment or involvement. Tears welled in Elle's eyes; she tasted the saltwater down her cheeks.

"Did you know all this at the casino?" she asked Erik.

"Bits and pieces. I had no idea what he was involved in. Certainly not the trio at the casino. Or what he was doing with the money orders he sent back home. I thought he was supporting his family or something."

Erik's dark eyes moistened.

"You missed him, Elle. He flew back to Manila to testify last year."

His boyfriend instinctively placed his hand over top of Erik's. The Swede boyfriend put his arm around Elle's shoulders.

When they rose to leave, Elle hugged Erik's man, then Erik himself. "Thank you for you," she whispered into Erik's ear. He had no idea what she meant but it didn't matter. She meant that his flipside was truly wondrous. Not undercover like Amado, funding weapons to overthrow a ruthless regime in his homeland. Not creepy like Russell counting cards and stalking redheads. Not like the fraudulent trio either. Erik's flipside was normal—delightful even. Elle laughed at the sheer innocence of Erik and released him from her arms.

VANCOUVER, CANADA
2013

MONEY WHEEL MAN

Russell and the redhead floated past Erik in the River Rock Casino Resort like he didn't exist, like Russell was too savvy for the money wheel. The redhead he was with was a smoke show. Russell was older, bigger, swollen up like a professional bodybuilder, but there was no mistaking the intensity of his rime blue eyes. Russell's eyes were a bleak window into a subhuman room. No surprise to Erik that Regrettable Russell would show up here at the Vancouver casino—he'd likely been banned from the casinos in Alberta.

The River Rock casino was packed this evening due to the high-stakes poker Tournament. Erik counted seven yachts docked in the marina on the Fraser River. He thought about Wayne and the retirement yacht he never got.

The blackjack tables rippled with excitement, roulette was at capacity, and the slot machines whirred and buzzed like a neon circus. Only Erik stood unoccupied except for the casual tourist that plunked down their last chip on the way over to the theatre show. He was free to watch Russell and the redhead circulate the posh floor of the 4-Diamond resort.

Erik saw the casino manager, Rosette Kwong, surveying the gaming floor from the second-storey balcony. He was grateful to Rosette. She'd taken him in decades back when he needed a job. He'd been with her so long now that he often forgot that she was his boss and not his poker-playing buddy on their days off—a perk of his long-standing employment. Erik rode the straight road after leaving the Alberta casino, though he still spiked his Black Russians with French Vanilla Vodka in the lounge after his casino shifts. He hadn't gone that straight.

He was in touch with Amado and his partner J-Mar, whom he hoped to meet one day if they ever came to Canada. He had his own flipbook calendar of past lovers, including his ex-wife, who had passed through with their son last year enroute to the Calgary Stampede. Aloof, his ex-wife eyed him up and down in the Vancouver airport, deciding if he was worthy of her forgiveness. When their now-adult son burst forward and hugged Erik around the waist like the kid Erik had left behind, he knew he'd been pardoned.

Russell and the redhead walked the perimeter of the Salon Privé where the high limit gaming tables were in full swing. The redhead was high limit material in a black backless dress, but Russell with his vintage leather jacket and Ed Hardy jeans looked like he was too superior to dress up. Still the same haughty Russell that Erik remembered.

Erik watched them circle back to the regular blackjack tables. Russell could wager good money at the lower limit table, and he'd be less likely to attract the attention of the casino manager. He and the redhead sat down at a table populated by a group of pensioners. After a couple of shoes, the pensioners vacated the table.

Russell and the redhead took over and played all seven squares.

On his dinner break, Erik was tempted to swing by their table to see how they were doing. He didn't want Russell to recognize him, so he wandered upstairs to the designated smoking balcony. The night air was warm and humid. Rosette was also on her dinner break.

"How are you doing, Erik?" Rosette asked in between bites of her Caesar salad while checking messages on her phone. She could do more things in five minutes than Erik could manage in an entire day. He watched her with admiration. Erik pulled a Marlboro out of his pack and offered her one. She accepted the cigarette and a light from Erik.

"Good poker tournament tonight?" Erik asked, directing his smoke away from her Caesar salad.

"Yes, a stellar turnout. Should be lucrative. Lots of high rollers. Good for business."

He hesitated mentioning Russell. As much as he harboured a strong dislike for the card counter, Russell knew the reason for Erik's abrupt departure from the Calgary casino—the stolen tips he'd wandered away with in the dark of night. He didn't want to risk that getting back to Rosette.

"Think you've got some card counters in tonight," Erik said, without saying how or why he knew that.

"Oh yeah?" Rosette narrowed her eyes in the direction of the high limit salon. "The Privé?"

"No, the regular tables."

"Let's go have a look, shall we?"

Rosette got up and stubbed her cigarette out. It was a game she and Erik often played— spot the card counter, pick out the dealers that were padding their tips, pinpoint the roulette player who'd added chips to the winning number when the dealer's back was turned. Erik was particularly good at this game. Gambling had been legal in Alberta long before BC legislated its own casinos, after all. Erik brought with him a wealth of subversive gambler and dealer behavior that he shared with Rosette, though she'd never asked him specifically where he'd worked. He could have worked in Vegas or Atlantic City, or the casinos further east in Ontario. They walked back into the casino and stood gazing over the stream of blackjack tables shored up with players. Rosette stood inside the pit watching until Erik had to go back to the money wheel.

"Come tell me when you find them," Erik said. She searched around in her pants pocket like she was looking for something, then pulled out her middle finger. Erik laughed.

Rosette's face was an intense, focussed beam of sharp light. She looked for the usual suspects. Players with high denomination chips in front of them. Players that rarely spoke or even acknowledged the other players at the table. A team of players who took over an entire table were clearly not playing for leisure. Players that signalled each other when the count was up. She surveyed the tables and her staff but saw nothing out of the ordinary. Players won, players lost.

She glanced over at Erik on the money wheel and followed his eyes. Two players at the end of the pit had the entire blackjack table locked up. That was interesting. Why not play the Salon Privé for high rollers? Erik winked at Rosette. She watched the table from behind.

"Cut off two decks this time," the pit boss ordered the dealer. The dealer complied. Russell raised his brow at the redhead in the backless dress. He didn't have to know who the casino manager was, but he could feel his or her presence on the floor. The redhead raised her drink unsteadily in the air like she was drunk.

"Thish square ish for you," she slurred. She placed a bet on the square for the dealer.

"Thank you, ma'am."

The dealer dealt the hands, then pulled a blackjack and scooped up their chips.

"So much for your tips," the redhead joked and ordered another drink from the cocktail server. Russell didn't react. He seemed preoccupied with other things. He watched the cards carefully. Halfway through the shoe, Russell raised his bets to the maximum, as did the redhead. He knew it was likely his last hand on this table, at this casino, in this province. The dealer busted her hand and paid them out. The pit boss ordered more chips for the tray again. Russell and the redhead had more chips than the dealer. Rosette strolled back inside the pit and stood next to the table.

"How are we doing tonight, folks?" she asked casually.

She didn't fool Russell. He knew she was the casino manager because the dealer and the pit boss looked categorically terrified at Rosette's big boss presence.

Russell didn't look at her. The redhead lifted her beautiful face and laughed like she was wildly drunk. Rosette glanced at the cocktail server for confirmation. He shook his head and set her fresh drink down on the River Rock coaster.

"Ginger ale," the cocktail server mouthed at Rosette. A shrewd card counter ploy that Rosette was familiar with thanks to Erik.

Rosette looked at their win fold of chips, which was easily over the ten-thousand-dollar mark. She was required by law to ask the players for identification at this threshold. They all knew it. Russell still refused to acknowledge her.

"Sir, I'm going to need your identification." Rosette felt her patience waning. The redhead slammed her ginger ale back in one shot. She pulled out her driver's licence and waved it around. Rosette passed it to the pit boss who ran it through their system. She wasn't flagged. Rosette waited for Russell to do likewise.

Russell rammed his stacked chips towards the dealer in a

messy pile.

"Cash me out." No please, no thank you, no eye contact with Rosette.

The pit boss rolled his eyes at Rosette. Russell could have let the dealer pull the stacks in to count them.

"Cash him out," Rosette commanded. The dealer restacked his chip, then verified the amount.

"Eighteen thousand, four hundred and twelve dollars," the dealer confirmed.

Rosette and the pit boss waited for Russell to push the twelve-dollar chips back toward the dealer as a tip, but he didn't. He pocketed the chips. The redhead shot up from her plush velvet stool like she wasn't drunk anymore. No one was surprised at her sudden sobriety. Russell's face was blood red. He could take his chips to the cashier, but he'd still have to show ID. The house had him between a hard place and a River Rock ball-buster. The redhead couldn't cash them in either, because they knew she was with Russell.

"Fuck you," Russell said under his breath.

"I beg your pardon, sir?"

Russell stomped across the luxurious palm tree carpet towards the cashier cage. The redhead followed. Rosette took a shortcut through the pit and waited by the cashier cage, smiling like a viper. Russell stopped mid-stride and glared at Rosette.

"Why don't you go fuck yourself?" he yelled at her. "And you too, you Dutch fag." Russell turned to Erik on the money wheel.

Erik shrugged. He'd been called worse. Russell *had* noticed him on the way in. *What a slick bastard,* Erik thought. Two Captain America-sized security men descended upon Russell and escorted him out the gold doors towards the dark waters of the Fraser River. The redhead shook her head at Erik, as if to say she was sorry Russell was such an asshole.

The security men waited until the fine-looking redhead caught up with Russell before leaving. Russell, with his pocket full of uncashed chips, was in no mood to enjoy the scenic boulevard.

Outside the casino in the designated smoking area, Rosette and Erik enjoyed a quick Marlboro.

"Where do you know him from, *you Dutch fag*?" Rosette asked, a wry smile on her lips.

Erik laughed. He'd let Rosette think what she wanted; that Russell was yet another ex-lover from Erik's ever-expanding Rolodex. Better that than outing himself as a former corrupted blackjack dealer from the Calgary casinos. He let Rosette have the last word. She'd get it one way or the other.

Russell and the redhead circled back to the front entrance of the River Rock casino. The poker tournament was on a break, and people were lined up outside for the late show at the theatre. Russell spotted a young woman dressed in a shimmering gold mini dress with an older man on her arm. The man, like Russell, was unreasonably jacked. No doubt that this man had to fight his way out of precarious situations as well.

"Try them," Russell instructed the redhead. She sidled up to the couple.

"Borrow a smoke?" she asked. The young woman in the shimmering dress had glassy eyes and track marks on her arms. She offered Verna one.

"Are you playing?" the redhead asked.

"Maybe," the man said, running his wary eyes over the redhead. "Why?"

"Think you could cash some chips in for me?"

"Why don't you cash them?"

"I got kicked out."

"Sure," the jacked man said. The redhead gave them each nine thousand in chips, just below the ten-thousand-dollar mark. No identification would be required.

"That's a good night," the older man said before leaving the theatre lineup with the young woman. They disappeared inside the casino while Russell hung back, far away from the security cameras. The redhead smoked her cigarette. After three more cigarettes, the couple still hadn't resurfaced. Russell paced in the parking lot. Neither he nor the redhead could venture back inside.

After a full hour, the couple swaggered out of the casino with cocktail glasses in their hands. A fluorescent blue liquid swirled inside.

"Finish them or leave them, folks," the man at the security desk told them. They opted to finish their cocktails at the security stand. To the outside eye, they resembled a lucky couple who'd had a fantastic night at the casino. Which they'd had. The redhead slid over.

"Have you got my money?" she asked the couple quietly.

"What money, honey?" the young woman slurred loudly. Only hers was an authentic slur—she reeked of cheap alcohol. The security guard perked up and didn't take his eyes off the three of them. He could spot a potential dust-up a kilometer away. The redhead glanced back at Russell. He started towards them but then stopped when the older man pulled his suit jacket back casually to reveal a concealed weapon. The redhead slunk back to Russell. Both stood watching while the couple chatted with the security guards. It was evident that they weren't going anywhere until Russell and the redhead left.

"Bad pick," the redhead told Russell. The couple raised their cocktail glasses at them.

"Shut the fuck up."

Russell was in no mood to be placated. He'd find a way to cash what little he had left, maybe exchange chips with a player from another casino. He'd at least get his buy-in back. But he was damn sure if he saw Erik again, he'd make amends on his Dutch bastard face.

CALGARY, CANADA
2017

PHOENIX RISING

Sunlight streams in through the window of Jeliane's childhood bedroom. She's back at her parents. Her mother closes the curtains. Within a matter of seconds, her breathing eases into sleep. She sleeps a full day and night. The following morning, rising like a Phoenix from the ashes, Jeliane has a plan. She's tired of capitulating to the patriarchy. She's tired of being scared, she's tired of men like Russell. She is Betty Friedan, Simone de Beauvoir. She is the third wave of feminism.

"Can I borrow your Honda, mum?" she asks.

"Where are you off to?" her mother asks, then remembers that Jeliane is an adult and needn't tell her mother her whereabouts.

"The university," Jeliane says.

"Be careful," her mother says, relieved that her daughter is at home and back at school, away from the reach of Regrettable Russell.

Jeliane parks her mother's Honda in the middle of the 5600 block in Varsity Acres. She watches the comings and goings on the suburban street. The next day, she choses a different location, repeating the process. They go to work, come home, swing their excited children over their heads, mow their lawns, take out the recycling, drink IPAs or mom wine on their decks. Jeliane surveys a different block each day, waiting for Russell to raise his ugly head.

On day six, she sees Russell in the living room window of his aunt's house. There is no mistaking his face from the front page of the *Calgary Herald*. She slides down in her mother's car. Russell paces back and forth past the living room window like a caged animal. *Right*, she thinks. *He's got an ankle bracelet. He is a caged animal.*

If they can't find the redhead's body, he might get off. Jeliane needs to find something to trip Russell up. He is slick but not infallible. No doubt, the police have searched the premises. An older woman comes around the side of the house. The aunt, no doubt. She's small and stringy, but her muscles are lean and veiny like a yoga addict.

Jeliane waits and watches over the next few days in her mother's Honda.

Each day at the same time, the mullet aunt climbs into her Chevy truck and disappears until well after dark. Must work a late shift somewhere. Russell remains in the house.

Elle drives down the back alley and parks. She examines the last known picture of the redhead via the CCTV footage on the front page of the *Calgary Herald*, takes note of her silk blouse, rhinestone bracelet, and black pearl earrings.

Jeliane removes her orange Nikes and gets out of the car.

The back of the aunt's house is dark, but coloured light flickers from the living room television. No porch light on. To be sure, Jelaine tosses a pinecone towards the back door. No motion sensor. No dog that she's seen.

The basement windows are regulation size, which makes it easy for Jeliane to slip through. She tests the latch on the window. Locked. She moves to the next window. Also locked. The third one on the side of the house isn't. She opens the window and waits. No alarms. No security cameras on this side of the house either, only at the front door. She's been careful to park her mother's Honda out of the scope of the front camera. She's a quick study who has watched far too many murder series.

Jeliane slithers through the side window and stands in the dim basement. She waits while her eyes adjust to the dark. It's an entire suite. She spies an unmade bed in the other room. Someone lives down here and she's sure it isn't the lamb of an aunt. In her two weeks of surveillance, the aunt has never gone downstairs.

Russell lives down here. She hears voices from upstairs. *Has the aunt come back already*? No, it's voices on the television. Women's voices that she recognizes from the same Netflix series she and her parents are watching. *Orange is the New Black*. The combination of prison and criminal chatter make her acutely aware that she's six feet beneath a woman killer.

Jeliane doesn't know what she's looking for, but she thinks the police might have missed something. She rummages through his bedside table. Nothing in the tables or in his dresser. Maybe he's preparing to flee the country? If he gets convicted, he's looking at serious prison time. Jeliane knows she must find something and that her life depends on it. She peers around the dark basement suite, then spots the huge glass tank on the far wall. Not Tiny! How did she miss that?

Russell shifts in his chair above her head. Jeliane cups her hands around the side of her phone and turns on the flashlight. The narrowed beam gives her just enough light. She skates across the cool linoleum and shines her light on the tank. Not Tiny stirs inside and flicks its licorice-black tongue against the glass. The python's massive black and tan body is coiled around elongated white eggs that are larger than Jeliane's hand. Baby pythons. Snakelets.

Jeliane runs her phone light over the enclosure. A vibration up her body tells her what the police might have missed. No one is going to search a python's cage, especially a police officer who doesn't get paid enough to risk death by snake.

"He's a nasty bastard," Jeliane whispers to Not Tiny. The python moves sidewise to wrap her muscled body protectively around her eggs. She knocks her water dish over in the process. The phone light glints off something buried in the sand beneath the overturned water dish. Jeliane doesn't have to see the full black earring to know it belongs to the redhead. *Murderers do not watch murder series* she decides. If they did, then they wouldn't be stupid enough to save souvenirs from their victims. He's a fucking cliché.

She undoes the metal clasp on the top of the snake tank. If she can distract the snake, she might be able to retrieve the earring. What if she gets bit and Russell finds her paralyzed on his aunt's cool linoleum? She knows Russell won't hesitate to make her go missing as well. Jesus fuck, can she do this? Her future depends on it. She lifts the glass lid of the tank gently. The snake spirals its massive head toward the top of the tank. She drops the lid with a sharp thud and holds her breath in panicky silence.

Above her, Russell rises from his chair. Did he hear her? Hear the tank lid? She listens for his footsteps. He crosses the living room. The toilet flushes and water whooshes down the pipe next to her, which further panics her. Then nothing. No movement from above. That more than anything terrifies her. She trains her light on the snake and watches in horror as Not Tiny glides to her overturned water dish and swallows the black pearl earring. *Christ almighty*, do pythons eat everything in sight? Could they digest pearl and metal, the last known remnant of a redhead?

Russell's footsteps are headed in her direction. She looks wildly at Not Tiny. She forgot to lock the clasp on the snake tank. She imagines Not Tiny's cold, dry body wrapped around her bare ankles.

Russell descends the basement stairs. Jeliane dives through the regulation window, skinning both knees on the metal frame. She doesn't bother to close the window, just sprints in the black along the cotoneasters to her mother's car. She starts the Honda and floors it in sock feet down the gravelled alley. She passes the aunt's truck as she speeds recklessly down the street.

"Slow the fuck down!" the aunt yells at Jeliane through the open window of her Chevy truck. It takes Jeliane four blocks to slow the fuck down and calm her drumming heart. She cups her bleeding, skinned kneecaps in her hands.

MANILA, PHILIPPINES 1988-2022

UNTIL

All eyes widened as Amado Barcelona entered the packed Manila courtroom dressed in his Fall Guy uniform. Pale blue shirt, navy trousers and his Sunday best shoes as a pakyu to the Marcoses. The Crying Lady and Lina Santos were flanked on all sides by the prosecutor's security team. The women were dressed from head to leather pumps in brilliant yellow. President Corazon Aquino and her mother-in-law were dressed in yellow blazers and matching pants. The pair nodded at Lina Santos as they passed by. Lina bowed her head in renewed grief. Rolando was in her mind and in her stinging heart. She felt his presence as surely as if he walked beside her. J-Mar in his airport uniform took a seat in the gallery next to the same foreign correspondent that he'd come across at the Rizal Park rally. The two men looked at each other in recognition. Grim acknowledgement spread across both their faces.

The world's eyes were focussed on this new trial. Imelda Marcos was glued to her television while former Philippine President

Ferdinand Marcos lay shivering down the hall in his Hawaiian bed. His body was ailing, dying, rejecting the kidney his son Bongbong had donated to him shortly after the assassination of Ninoy Aquino and the murder of the pig farmer. Hence the reports that the Iron Butterfly was the real mastermind and not her failing husband.

General Perez and his team of dark-suited lawyers paled at the entrance of the holy trinity. Not the father, the son and the holy ghost, but the Baggage Handler, the Crying Lady and the Wife of the Pig Farmer. Add to that the tall soldier dressed in the same military uniform he'd worn on the tarmac. The smell of gunpowder embedded in the very fabric of his camouflage shirt permeated the courtroom. The jurors' faces pivoted towards the smell. His fifteen comrades glowered at him as he took his place next to the holy trinity. Contrition was on his mind—what happened to him did not matter. Only the holy trinity mattered.

"*You* picked up my husband," Lina Santos said repeatedly over the course of that year and a half trial, where she testified again and again. After each examination and cross examination, the defense lawyers realized her story would not waver with each new piece of the murder puzzle that surfaced.

"You," she said, pointing her forefinger at General Perez. "*You* picked up my husband."

"How could you be certain at four in the morning?" the defense lawyers pressed.

"Because I was scared. Because I knew it was important."

She cited the exact make and model of the four-door car; the exact time, which was corroborated by her neighbour and his large wife in her rubber shoes. The man who'd found the money beneath the pigs' feed and held onto it, then distributed it amongst the other poor farmers. The large woman who harvested the yellow, fragrant ylang-ylang and sold the blooms at the market for Lina in case she returned to the farm.

"He lit my husband's cigarette," Lina continued. "That's how I saw his face at four in the morning." Lina pointed again, which had the effect of a shot fired. General Perez flinched back in his swivel chair, where his neutral face faltered and betrayed him. His defense lawyers looked dispirited.

Later that year, the Crying Lady studied the blown up black and white photos that Ken Kashiwahara had released. Five soldiers were positioned on the air stairs. A man in a white safari suit was in their midst.

"That one pulled the trigger," the Crying Lady said. She singled out the soldier directly behind Ninoy Aquino in the photograph, then matched his face to the live soldier in the courtroom. An audible gasp from the jurors and the galley. President Corazon and Aquino's mother lowered their heads and pressed tissues to their leaking eyes until they could compose themselves. The new trial was like a band-aid that had ripped off their scabbed grief and made it fresh again. The two women hugged each other. This was the day they'd waited five years for.

In the gallery, J-Mar patted Ken Kashiwahara's forearm.

"Good capture," he said about the photograph. Ken squeezed J-Mar's wrist in response. They purposely sat beside one another day in, day out. Jim Laurie and Ken Kashiwahara kept nodding throughout the Crying Lady's testimony. The defense lawyers took potshots at the Crying Lady, describing her as an embezzler of money and a passer of fraudulent cheques. The jurors looked dubious. Unlike the first trial where the Crying Lady had left the courtroom in shame, this time she held her head high. She knew who would testify after her. Amado Barcelona watched her with his gold eyes on fire. In the fashionable Makiki Heights region of Honolulu in a two-million-dollar house on beachfront property, Ferdinand

Marcos drew his final breath in the fall of 1989. The trial prevailed. His wife Imelda Marcos was not with him at the time of his death.

Amado Barcelona gazed at the crowded gallery from the witness stand. He'd worn his airport uniform every single day, and the judge did not forbid it.

"It's his right," the judge told the defense lawyers when they kicked up a fuss.

"It's prejudicing the jurors," the defense lawyers argued.

"I work at the airport," Amado told the judge. He'd done so since returning home.

"I will allow it," the judge said, cutting the dog shark team of defense lawyers off at the gills. General Perez glared at Amado from the defense table.

"Where were you when Ninoy Aquino was shot?" the prosecutor asked.

"I was fifty feet away on my pull cart," Amado said.

"What did you see?"

The defense council protested the generality of the question.

"Specifics," the judge instructed the prosecutor.

"Did you see and hear the shot that killed Opposition Leader Benigno 'Ninoy' Aquino?"

"I saw exactly what she saw," Amado said, motioning towards the Crying Lady. He then pointed at the terrified soldier seated on the bench behind General Perez. "That soldier fired his pistol into the back of Ninoy Aquino's head on the air stairs."

"Was General Perez also present on the tarmac that day?"

The prosecutor turned toward the General. In the previous trial, the same sixteen soldiers seated behind him had testified that they had not seen the General that day.

"Yes, he was standing next to the air stairs," Amado said, confirming the Crying Lady's testimony.

"How did you know how many shots?"

"The sixteen shots matched my smoke ring record," Amado said. "I count things."

His eyes filled. There was no joy in recounting the death of a cordial pig farmer.

Lina Santos held her gold cross tight in her fist. The cunning General, who knew what was going to happen before it happened, dropped his intense gaze. He knew his fate before the jury had even decided. He knew he was going to prison for the rest of his life once the prosecutors and defense team had sorted out whose guns and whose bullets were present in the body of Rolando Galman on the runway. Life in prison also for the fifteen of the soldiers.

The tall soldier who testified for the prosecution was sentenced to eight years in prison. It was a small price to pay for his wretched part. No Nuremberg defense would excuse him. Nonetheless, Lina Santos would forgive him. So would President Corazon Aquino. His penance would last his whole life.

President Corazon Aquino and her mother-in-law walked across the courtroom and hugged Lina Santos and Amado Barcelona and the Crying Lady like they were family. The Crying Lady who'd cried for everyone over those five long years cried for herself now. Lina Santos cried for her pig farmer husband. Amado Barcelona cried in exhaustion and relief. He would need no more humming dryers. He would sleep like his mother's baby once more.

When they exited the courtroom, the zealous press descended upon President Corazon Aquino.

"They have not convicted the mastermind," Corazon Aquino told the press. Ken Kashiwahara and Jim Laurie at her side nodded in agreement.

"But the mastermind, I believe, is already resting in peace," a journalist ventured.

The President would not further disparage Ferdinand Marcos's death. Her mother-in-law held her arm and remained mute.

Ninoy Aquino had been resting in peace for some five years now in the Manila Memorial Park in Parañaque. The ceremonial graveyard was reserved for heroes and political leaders. Dictators needn't apply. On November 18, 2016, however, after a secret court ruling, the remains of Ferdinand Marcos were moved and interned there despite fierce opposition from the Aquino family and half of the one hundred and three point seven million Filipino people. They had not forgotten the darkest period in their Philippine history.

Regardless, killed and killer were laid six feet under in the same graveyard.

Newly elected President Bongbong Marcos in 2022 would be called upon by the people to apologize for his father's treacherous years.

"Move on," he'd tell the people. "We have nothing to apologize for."

Rolando Galman was laid to rest at God knows where. Perhaps General Perez knew, but after his lifetime conviction, he wasn't forthcoming with the information. Neither was God. No ylang-ylang blossoms for Rolando's grave, no grave to speak of despite Lina Santos's best efforts to locate his remains. He'd wander the earth without her until she no longer walked among the living. Then they'd walk together.

CALGARY, CANADA
2017

ROCK STAR

In the darkened basement suite on the 5600 block of Varsity Acres, Russell lies restless in his bed. He can't sleep. He can't shake the redhead from his mind, or the trial he faces on Monday morning. His mullet-haired aunt is asleep in her bed above.

In the other room, Tiny coils her African Rock python body around her newly hatched snakelets. All but one have emerged from their flexible, leathery shells. She tightens her coils lovingly around her shivering snakelets, then tucks them beneath the heat lamp for extra warmth. She's a rock star mother. Tiny slips out of the open tank that the blonde woman forgot to lock. The black pearl earring is in her belly along with sixteen mice, four rats and a celebratory chick. She slithers in rectilinear locomotion, the straight line of her eight-foot body moving across the cold linoleum to her beloved master's bedroom. He might need protection too.

CALGARY, CANADA 2017

WHO WORE WHAT IN THE COURTROOM?

On Monday morning, the Calgary courtroom is a packed house with three hundred spectators and twelve conservatively dressed jurors. Elle sits in the gallery alongside her Swede husband.

Her daughter Jeliane wears a black toque pulled low over her white, blonde hair and orange neon Nikes. She is hard to miss. Jeliane's barista bro Matt has on a fresh t-shirt that reads *I work hard so my cat can have nice things*. The air in the courtroom is charged.

Russell Braydon's defense lawyer cranes his head towards the brass inlaid doors, as do the three detectives.

Neither Russell nor the aunt are present yet. The lawyer talked to Russell on Friday night, advising him to wear his best suit. "A blue one if you've got it. And shave. Get your aunt to trim your hair. Get your aunt to trim her hair. Be rested, don't drink, don't come in hungover. Be on your best behavior. Your life depends on that first glimpse the jury gets of you. Lose some of that haughtiness. Practice your poker face."

The lawyer knows Russell won't have a problem with that. The guy rarely shows any emotion. Like a reptile, Russell blinks periodically. Everything that matters, matters in those first four seconds.

While they wait for the defendant, the people in the gallery crane their heads to appreciate the spectacle that Russell Braydon has put together. Players and dealers that Elle hasn't seen in decades. Rude Rudy sits next to a lovely woman dressed in a lemon cashmere sweater. Billy Jacked is there wearing an actual shirt and tie. George Apple strides past with a new woman on his arm and likely a new car in the parking lot. George looks surprised. He hasn't seen Elle in decades.

"You used to be such a nice girl," he teases her.

The woman on George's arm narrows her eyes. Elle laughs. George Apple is the congenial, older brother she never had. The wife doesn't have to worry about her. Moose sits higher up in the gallery with an older, recognizable Liv Taylor pressed next to him. The enduring surprise of Liv's clear, violet eyes is still there. There is no residual evidence of Russell that Elle can see. Elle realizes that they must be a couple. Russell's ex is Moose's current. You can't make this shit up.

"Baby Cakes," Moose mouths at her. Elle half expects Wayne to waft down from the rafters in a West Coast yacht. The entire casino circus is here to witness Regrettable Russell get his comeuppance. Elle searches the courthouse for her casino comrade-in-arms, Amado and Erik. She'd give her left eye to see them again.

Jeliane elbows her mother in the ribs when Verna's family enters. The courtroom goes quiet.

A detective strides across the floor to the gallery.

"Is that you on the CCTV footage?" the detective asks Jeliane.

Jeliane glances at her mother. Elle waits for Jeliane to respond. Jeliane nods.

"We need to talk."

"I'll be here," Jeliane says. She will not shrink away from Russell again. Russell will not be free to murder women in broad daylight in the front seat of his SUV. The detective gives Jeliane his card and crosses the room. Jeliane cranes around and spots the single nurse mother from her Varsity Acres basement suite.

"Where's Bernard?" she asks.

"He's at home with our children."

The two women smile at the beauty of that.

The judge enters the courtroom. The gallery and jurors rise and sit down and wait some more. Russell's defense lawyer is fixated on the bronze inlaid doors as if they are willing Russell to miraculously appear. No Russell. After another ten restless minutes, a police officer rushes into the courtroom to speak with the defense lawyer. The defense lawyer asks to approach the bench along with the bewildered prosecution.

The judge motions for the police officer and the court stenographer to also approach. No one knows what's going on.

Russell has likely fled the country. Jeliane leans forward and looks intently at her mother. Elle reaches out and squeezes her daughter's delicate wrist. Jeliane's father holds one hand while Matt holds her other.

The judge pounds his gavel for silence.

The jurors lean forward in their wood chairs. The defense lawyer and prosecutor return to their respective tables.

The stenographer passes the judge his laptop. Everyone in the courtroom pitches forward to hear the judge.

He reads with the face of a consummate poker player. There is no flicker of amazement across his puffy face, no twitch on his pink lips, no crook of his thick brow.

"This trial is dismissed," the judge says. "The defendant Russell Braydon has been declared deceased."

Elle and Jeliane hold their breath at the same time. The judge switches gears.

"Time of death—" the judge continues, although he doesn't get to finish before Verna's family jumps up from their seats. They cry out in pain and disbelief while the courtroom remains deathly silent.

On Tuesday morning, Elle rises early and goes out to retrieve the newspaper. Jeliane and her husband are asleep in their respective rooms. Matt stayed over and is splayed on the living room sofa. She tiptoes past him and sits on the front step. The sun is a soft yellow rising above the line of oak trees on the horizon. When the elastic band is pulled off, the newspaper uncoils across her bare knees. On the front page of the *Calgary Herald* on August 9, 2017, Elle reads:

> Nefarious Calgary card counter Russell Braydon died of asphyxia after his 2.4 metre (8ft) pet African rock python wrapped herself around him, a shocked Calgary courtroom heard yesterday.
>
> Russell Braydon was charged with the first-degree murder of his gaming partner Verna Jones. Her body has not yet been found. Mr. Braydon died from asphyxiation in his bed at his aunt's home in the 5600 block of Varsity Acres in Calgary on the morning of 8 August 2017.
>
> His pet—a female African rock python named "Tiny"—was found near his body, out of its glass enclosure. Fourteen

hatchlings were also recovered from the basement suite.

Calgary coroner Andrea Meyers said there was no doubt Mr. Braydon died because of contact with Tiny. She recorded a verdict of misadventure. She made it clear she did not believe the snake had been aggressive towards its owner, but that the most likely scenario was that the reptile had been coiling around him in a protective way.

The African rock python and her recent hatchlings have been relocated to the Wilder Institute at the Calgary Zoo.

Elle folds the newspaper in half and watches the sun get higher in the eastern sky. She saunters back into the house. She'll wait for the others to wake. At some point soon, she and Jeliane will visit Tiny at the Calgary Zoo.

VANCOUVER, CANADA
2017

UNTIL WE MEET AGAIN

Amado Barcelona also boards a Boeing 767 at the Ninoy Aquino International Airport bound for Canada. He makes his way through the Vancouver International Airport past the traditional post-and-beam longhouse that reaches the glass and metal skylights. Past the seventeen-foot cedar spindles of two eagles carved around two men with outstretched arms. Past the Jade Canoe, a monumental six-ton bronze sculpture that features a single human surrounded by trickster creatures in a jade-green patina. Amado, in his international jet lag, fails to properly understand any of it.

Amado takes the Skytrain Downtown. He has no luggage other than his *Millennium Falcon* backpack. He closes his eyes and does not open them until the train announces Yaletown. Amado exits and walks the long hot blocks to Denman Street on English Bay. It's not much different than his homeland in the salty brine of the Pacific. He clutches a letter in his hand and scans the street address. The street is teeming with people and iced coffees and palabok noodles and fruit smoothies. Amado hasn't eaten in sixteen hours.

At the Falafel King, Amado rechecks the address on the letter. He climbs up to the second floor above. The hallway is narrow and without lights. At the last door, he knocks and waits. Nothing. He knocks again. His heart pounds in his ears. He's come all this way. He twists the glass doorknob and finds it locked. He lies against the locked door in exhaustion. His plans include only this. He has no back up.

He hears the door clank below him, then the heavy footfalls of someone mounting the stairs. Amado turns and waits for whatever comes. The figure disappears into another apartment. Amado almost cries. He knocks once more on the locked door.

Erik opens the door to find the sad eyes of a lost man. His own slick greying hair is dishevelled. He's just woken up. He stares at Amado like he is an apparition— a spirit from his dubious past that he'd long let go.

Amado can't stop the tears running down his face. Erik takes him in his Dutch arms. His casino comrade in arms. The light of his pale gold eyes in the dark hall.

Acknowledgements

In my twenties, I worked the casinos in Calgary with a friend who'd emigrated from the Philippines. Blackjack and roulette dealers, we all rolled around together, saw each other six days a week, took breaks together, and went out for drinks and food after work. This went on for a couple of years. Then one day the attorney general department in charge of gaming escorted my friend out of the casino. I had no idea why. When I found years later what he'd done, I was intrigued. When I found out *why* he did it, I was gobsmacked. While I was fighting with my then-boyfriend over who would clean the bathtub and iron *his* shirts for the work week, my friend was involved in something much more clandestine. I coupled his story with that of a blackjack dealer that became a world-renowned card counter in the early days of Alberta casinos. When I found out what he did decades later, I was horrified. The flipside of people that you can't anticipate.

This novel is the result of a short story by the same name, which garnered me a Canada Council grant and won silver in the Alberta Magazine Awards this past year. Big thanks to the Canada Council for supporting writers in their ongoing endeavors.

Along with my in-depth research on the Philippines, I was fortunate to interview an amazing group of people who experienced the revolution firsthand in the mid-80s. Some were politically active during that time. I'm indebted to them for their patience in answering my many questions and giving me the context of those tumultuous twenty years of martial law. I'm grateful for their reading of this manuscript and suggestions. While they have chosen not to be named due to the current political state in the Philippines, they are brave, good people, and I am the benefactor of their wealth and generosity in helping this book come to life. They know who they are, and I thank them.

A book that was particularly valuable was *An Eyewitness History People Power: The Philippine Revolution of 1986* by Monina Allarye Mercado. Vintage news videos on YouTube were extremely influential in my research and emotional sensibility of this book. While this story reflects political history, characters and events have been altered to suit the story. Any inaccuracies are intentional and entirely mine.

Casino research involved past and present colleagues that were integral in helping me put the pieces together so long after the fact. I am obliged to Joe Chapple, Kevin Booth and others who have chosen not to be named. Again, they know that I am grateful for their time and insights and shared memories.

Early readers and crucial structural advice came via Paul Rasporich, Kai Rasporich, Seth Rasporich, Robyn Humphreys, and Laura Hagerman. Thank you to all of you, always. Your support and love are close to my heart.

Great Plains Press has been a joy to work with in allowing me absolute autonomy, what every writer wants. My biggest thanks go to my editor, Jean Marc Ah-Sen, writer extraordinaire himself with keen editorial eyes and a terrific mind for story flow. I feel like I should add him as co-writer instead of editor, haha. He's made this novel clean and clear and sharp. Thank you, Jean Marc. Thank you also to Catharina de Bakker for her sharp dedication to the written word.

And lastly, thank you to book readers near and far. You are the reason writers continue to persist. We are all beholden to all of you.

Praise for Catch You on the Flipside

"If gambling intrigue, bear attacks, and political kleptocracy are at all your pet subjects, this may be the book you've been waiting for." — Jean Marc Ah-Sen, author of *In the Beggarly Style of Imitation*

"Current, urgent and utterly convincing, Catch You on the Flipside ties corrupt, Marcos-era Philippines to boom-bust Calgary of the early 1980s. Lee Kvern's authentic, vividly drawn characters prove that everyone, peon or potentate, has an unexpected Side B." — Richard Cumyn, author of *This Lark of Stolen Time*

"Catch You On The Flipside is an international thriller that deftly draws together an assassination in Manila, the staff at a Calgary casino, and a stalked barista. The fresh deck of characters includes famous politicians, unlucky baggage handlers, nefarious gun toters, smoke show redheads, and idiosyncratic casino regulars. In crisp inimitable prose that shows she knows when to hold 'em and when to fold 'em, Lee Kvern deals round after round of suspense and asks: "If a butterfly flapped its wings in Calgary, would it set off a storm in the Philippines?" — Barb Howard, author of *Happy Sands*

"With this book, Lee Kvern gives us a thrilling ride, a delicious noir, both lush and intense. Each chapter is vividly wrought with a tension so palpable, the pages turn themselves. Spanning decades and continents, and with an epic scope and ensemble of characters, every reader is in for a vibrant experience!" — Bradley Somer, award-winning author of *Fishbowl* and *Extinction*